RATTLESNAKE ROCK

by

Angela Dorsey

Enchanted Pony Books

www.ponybooks.com

Copyright © Angela Dorsey 2011
www.angeladorsey.com

Original Title: Rattlesnake Rock
Cover Design: 2011 Marina Miller
Printed in the USA, 2011

ISBN: 978-0-9876848-8-2

Enchanted Pony Books
www.ponybooks.com

Horse Guardian Series

Dark Fire
Desert Song
Condor Mountain
Swift Current
Gold Fever
Slave Child
Rattlesnake Rock
Sobekkare's Revenge
Mystic Tide
Silver Dream
Fighting Chance
Wolf Chasm

Freedom Series

Freedom
Echo
Whisper

Whinnies on the Wind Series

Winter of Crystal Dances
Spring of the Poacher's Moon
Summer of Wild Hearts
Autumn in Snake Canyon
Winter of Sinking Waters
Spring of Secrets
Summer of Desperate Races
Autumn of the Angel Mare
Winter of the Whinnies Brigade

Angelica

Vivo. You must be strong. I know you are frightened but believe me when I tell you, you will not die here. There are many years in front of you still. I know it is difficult to understand, but I cannot pull you from this mud hole, no matter how much I long to. Another is meant to rescue you, one who will be very crucial to your survival and the survival of your herd. All I can do is stop you from sinking too deeply into the mud until she comes.

I know you cannot stand being trapped in this cold, sucking wetness, and your legs feel like they are stiffening in place. I understand how you hate being so helpless, so vulnerable.

But my dear Vivo, you must endure this. You must be patient and strong. Draw upon your reserves of fortitude. She who is coming will come soon. Be resilient, my love, and know I will not leave you.

Rosa

Rosa stroked the bay gelding on his glistening neck. "It feels so wonderful to be out, Ciervo," she enthused. "And we have all afternoon to do whatever we want." She leaned over her horse's neck and inhaled his scent, her heart burning within her chest. She loved Ciervo so much. He was the most awesome horse she'd ever met. So elegant and fast. It was no mystery as to why his name meant *deer*. She gripped his long, ebony mane, squeezed her calves against his bare sides, and the gelding leapt forward. His hooves skimmed over the desert as he wove surefooted between the cacti and sagebrush.

Ciervo had been Rosa's best friend for ages, long before her father, who worked as a ranch hand on Senor Garcia's ranch, had bought him from the ranch owner five years earlier. Even now, Rosa had a hard time believing Senor Garcia had sold the gelding simply because he was getting old. Ciervo was still perfectly healthy. When Rosa's dad went to talk to Senor Garcia about buying the horse for Rosa and her sister, Rina, he hadn't been a moment too soon. Senor Garcia had already arranged for Senor Domingo, the slaughterer, to come for the gelding. Luckily, Rosa's dad offered more money and Senor Garcia phoned the slaughterer to cancel.

Rosa would always be grateful to her dad for buying the stylish old gelding. She'd seen other horses taken away in the slaughterer's truck and it never failed to make her heart ache. Ever since Ciervo became hers, she'd tried to make Senor Garcia see the error in his thinking. She wanted him to understand that horses weren't just tools to be discarded, especially when the rancher could afford to retire all his old ranch horses. He was rich enough to let them live out their final years in peace.

But because she was too shy to speak to Senor Garcia, her methods had to be subtler. She made sure Ciervo always looked his best whenever the ranch owner would see him. She'd ask him to prance when she noticed the man's eyes following them. Senor Garcia always seemed to be aware of Ciervo too, usually with a frown on his face. But so far, her efforts hadn't been successful. The older horses were still sent away to be killed. Nor had her efforts stopped Senor Domingo, the horse slaughterer, from looking at Ciervo with greedy eyes whenever he came to the ranch.

Rosa crouched even lower over Ciervo's neck when they reached a brush-free spot and the gelding lengthened his stride. The last thing she wanted to think of today was of her fruitless efforts to reform Senor Garcia. It only made her feel sad and helpless. Especially since Bonita, the horse her father rode to do his work on the ranch, was nearing twenty, the retirement age set by Senor Garcia.

Rosa had met the beautiful sorrel mare on the day her family moved to the ranch. She'd been three, and Bonita ten. It was her first time on the back of a horse, and instead of feeling frightened at her great distance from the ground, Rosa felt exhilarated. She'd felt as if she could fly.

She tightened Ciervo's reins at the far edge of the clear patch and straightened on his bare back. With one ear pricked forward and the other back to hear her better, Ciervo fell into a rocking-horse canter, a gait that ate up the distance very quickly and smoothly. Rosa glanced back. The ranch was completely out of sight now. She and Ciervo were alone on the desert. At last!

Rosa loved being out on the beautiful Mexican desert, especially with Ciervo. There were so many things to do. They could search for lizards and other desert creatures, or ride into the foothills to explore the canyons. They could canter the five miles to the ocean and play in the surf, or go to her favorite thinking spot, Rattlesnake Rock. The massive black boulder never ceased to amaze her. It had balanced on its small end for centuries, perched at the edge of the bluff, high above the miles-long driveway. A streak of white quartz swirled up its surface, looking for all the world like a giant white snake sitting at the top of the rise, overlooking its domain.

Rosa drew a deep breath of desert-spiced air. She'd been dying to get out all week, but there had been too much work to do around home. It was branding time. For weeks, the ranch hands had been rounding up the cattle from Senor Garcia's vast lands, and then last week, they'd branded the calves – and there were hundreds of calves to brand. The ranch was a bustling, noisy hive of activity and her father was exhausted when he came home every night.

In addition to helping the ranch hands by running errands and carrying messages, Rosa had schoolwork to do, something that never ever seemed to change, no matter how many hours she spent studying. With her distance-education schooling, there always seemed too much to do, some assignment to finish and mail out, some chapter to read from a heavy, boring textbook. But finally, early that afternoon, she'd gotten the last of her assignments done for the week. She was free!

And today she had something special thing to do, something she'd been looking forward to all week. She wanted to check on the mustang herd she'd found hiding in the hills.

She'd found them a couple of weeks before, at the far end of the canyon situated in the northernmost corner of the ranch, the one called Lost Canyon. At first, she wondered if she should run them off. She knew how much Senor Garcia hated mustangs – they ate the sparse vegetation he wanted for his cattle – and she knew he'd round them up and sell them for slaughter if he found them.

After much thought, she decided to leave the twelve horses where they were. It was too risky to move them. Because of the cattle roundup, the ranch hands were roaming the massive property looking for stray cows and calves. Chances were too high that the mustangs, or their tracks, or even the dust they kicked up, would be noticed by one of the cattlemen. And there was another danger – with only her and Ciervo to herd them, the mustangs might run *toward* the ranch headquarters. They would be discovered for sure then, and that would be the end of them. Their best chance at survival, Rosa reasoned, was to stay at the back of Lost

Canyon and hope that none of the ranch hands would go there searching for cattle.

For one brief moment, Rosa had thought of telling her father about the mustangs. The way she figured it, if another of the other ranch hands was assigned to check the canyon, her father could offer to do it for him, and afterward say the canyon was empty. But in her heart, she knew she couldn't tell him. No matter what happened, neither her mother nor father could know about the horses. If the ranch owner discovered the herd and had even the slightest hint that her parents knew they were there and hadn't told him, they would immediately be fired. Then their whole family would have to leave their home, the little adobe house beneath the trees that Senor Garcia let them live in while her parents worked for him.

The horses will be all right anyway, Rosa reassured herself for what seemed the hundredth time. *No one ever goes to Lost Canyon, not even the cattle. I've never seen any sign of the longhorns there. And if the cows don't go there, why would the ranch hands even check it?*

Besides, Papa would've said something if they'd found a herd of wild horses. And now that the roundup's over, the horses will be safe for another year. I just want to double check that they're okay, that's all.

Senor Garcia

Senor Garcia grunted, leaned back in his plush leather chair, and placed his hands over his hard midriff. His eyes were beginning to ache. And no matter how he went over the numbers, it didn't make sense. The ranch hands swore they'd checked the entire ranch, yet there had to be some cattle still out there. The numbers just didn't add up.

The longhorns had been out grazing and giving birth to their calves, almost 500 mother cows in total. Most of the calves had been born by now and yet they only had about 800 cattle in their corrals. There should have been at least 950. One hundred and fifty missing? It was far too many.

Where could they be? Even the men he'd sent out last week to bring in the stragglers hadn't found them. They'd arrived back at the ranch headquarters that afternoon – with about 20 stray cows and calves.

He cursed under his breath. Maybe they were hiding in the foothills? Or worse, maybe there was a hole in the fence?

Either way, there was no getting around it. He'd have to send out more men, some to check the fences around the perimeter of his property and some to the more remote areas of the ranch, just in case the missing cattle were holed up in some hidden meadow.

First thing in the morning, he'd divide the men into teams and send them out. One hundred fifty cows didn't just disappear into thin air. They were out there somewhere – and come hell or high water, he was going to find them.

Rosa

The foothills came steadily nearer, their dry contours sharp against the intense azure sky. Ciervo was becoming hot and Rosa pulled him down to a running walk. They were close now. Soon they'd be in the shade created by the narrow canyon.

The first time she'd seen the wild herd, Rosa was relieved that they'd chosen Lost Canyon for their home. As a hiding spot, she couldn't have picked better herself. The canyon was long, narrow, and sloped down gently along its length. At the end, a short, sharp drop levelled off into a wide, natural pasture that was always greener than the rest of the ranch. Rainwater that ran down the canyon to pool in the meadow was the key to its lushness. She could imagine the meadow vivid and alive now, as if a green veil had been pulled across its brown-edged dryness. Rain had fallen just two days ago, the first good rain in almost three months. The meadow would be reviving with new tender grasses. She smiled. The mustangs would enjoy that.

There was one seriously negative thing about the hidden meadow, though. There was no escape route other than the long, narrow chasm leading into it. Anyone discovering the wild ones would also be blocking their escape, unless the mustangs mustered the courage to stampede past them, something Rosa couldn't see any mustang ever doing.

She reined Ciervo up a short rocky incline and between the rocky walls. A smile touched her lips when she saw there were no hoof prints in the dirt. No one had entered or left the canyon since the rain had fallen. Unless the horses had ventured out more than two days ago, they were still here.

She trotted and cantered Ciervo along the sandy-bottomed canyon until she saw a tall, thin stone protruding from the ground. A rocky spur jutted out near the top like a hooked beak. Rosa reined the gelding to stop, slid from his back, and slipped off his bridle. Ciervo was wearing his halter beneath, and Rosa quickly untied the lead rope secured around his neck. She clipped one end to his halter ring and tied the other around the rock, then hung the bridle on the rocky spur.

"I'll be back soon," she said and gave Ciervo a quick hug, then stroked his blazed face and kissed the swirl of hair in the center of his forehead. "You just rest here in the shade." He nickered to her, then sniffed at her jeans pocket. Rosa smiled. "You know me too well, amigo," she said and reached into her pocket to grab a handful of crushed oats. She held her hand flat so he could pick the grains from her palm, then stroked his dark neck and moved off.

She kept to the far right side of the canyon as she hurried along. It was growing late and if she wanted to make it home before supper as she'd promised her mother, she'd have to hurry. There was still the long ride back to the ranch. She had less than an hour to watch the wild ones.

She flattened herself against the wall just before the last turn and slowly peeked around. She could see a thin strip of the green meadow between canyon walls, but no horses. Crouching low, she ran to hide behind a large rock outcropping. She looked again. More pasture was visible, but still no horses. Did they leave before the rain came? Moving as soundlessly as possible, she dashed to hide behind a large rock nearer the canyon mouth. Slowly, she peered over the edge. From this viewpoint, she'd be able to see most of the wild meadow. Her eyes swept across the green expanse.

And there they were, standing in a huddle near the water hole!

The joyous expression on Rosa's face slowly seeped away when she noticed the mustangs weren't drinking. So why were they standing in such a tight bunch?

Then she noticed the colt at their hooves, lying in the water.

But that doesn't make sense, she thought. *Horses don't rest in water.*

With sudden alarm, she realized what was happening. The two-year-old colt was stuck. The rain had created a mud hole and he had walked into it, unaware.

I have to help him, she thought, and straightened without thinking. Palomino, pinto, chestnut, bay, and gray heads turned toward her as one. A second later, the herd was on the move. And the colt – the colt she remembered being white but who was now the color of mud – struggled like a mad thing, sinking deeper into the mire.

Angelica

Vivo, I must go with the others. It is important that you meet her alone. She cannot know I am here yet. You must befriend her without my help.

I know you are terrified. I can feel your fear blast against me like gale force winds. I know that what I ask of you seems impossible, insurmountable, infinitely hard, but please, Vivo, you must give this small human a chance. In fact, do not think of her as human, at least in the way you've been taught to think of humans. Think of her instead as simply another creature, with hopes and dreams, just as you have hopes and dreams.

I know it is difficult, Vivo, but you must believe me. Humans are not all bad, once you get to know them.

Senor Garcia

Senor Garcia walked along the pole fence, his critical eye running over his herds. He had to admit, he had very little to complain about this year other than the missing cattle. The longhorns his men had brought in were fat and their calves were healthy.

"Jose!" he called and beckoned to a wiry man on a big sorrel mare. "Come here."

Jose Fernandez galloped his horse to where Senor Garcia waited, and dismounted. He removed his dusty hat before he spoke. "Si, Senor?"

"We have some cow-calf pairs missing — quite a few, in fact. Any idea where they might be?" His hard eyes bored into his employee's.

Jose met Senor Garcia's glower with obvious effort. "We checked all the usual places, Senor."

"Well, then I suggest you check all the unusual places."

"Si, Boss." Jose's gaze dropped to the ground.

"Get four teams of two or three men each, ready to ride by morning. Each group goes a different direction. I want the foothills checked again and another team to head toward the beaches. The third team can go south and the fourth team can start to check the fences."

"Si, Senor." The ranch hand exhaled with relief when the ranch owner turned away.

"And Jose?" Senor Garcia wheeled around. "I've been meaning to ask you about that mare you ride. I think it's about time we got you on another horse, a young one."

Jose Fernandez looked at the mare standing patiently behind him and his breath quickened. "But Bonita's a good mare, Senor. She works hard and she's smart and fast. I'd like to keep ..."

"No, you need a younger horse," Senor Garcia interrupted him. Then he turned on his heel and stalked back toward the ranch office. His parting words floated back over his shoulder. "I'll assign you one of the new colts and call Senor Domingo next week."

Rosa

Rosa hardly looked at the mustangs galloping away from her. Her eyes were locked on the muddy colt. He was so frightened she could see the whites of his eyes, even from a distance. She had to help him. But how? She needed a rope to pull him out – and she had a rope!

Without wasting another moment, Rosa ran back down the canyon to fetch Ciervo and his lead rope. With Ciervo's help, she could pull the colt from the mud, *if* the rope was long enough, *if* she could get close enough to the mustang to put a halter on him, and *if* he didn't sink too deep into the muck first!

Ciervo snorted and jumped back when she burst around the corner. "Whoa, amigo," said Rosa in a soothing voice and slowed to a quick walk. She reached Ciervo and lifted the bridle from the stony hook. Within seconds, she had the halter off, the bridle on, and was astride his strong back with the halter and rope lying across his withers.

"Let's go," she said and squeezed the gelding's side. He jumped forward, impatient to be off. Swiftly they moved along the canyon floor and broke into the meadow. Two of the mustangs had covered half the distance back to the colt, but when they saw Rosa and Ciervo, they spun around and galloped back to huddle with the others against the canyon wall, their heads held high in fear.

A high-pitched scream rang through the air and Rosa looked back at the colt. He was struggling again, and his jerky attempts to escape were making him sink faster.

"What are we going to do, Ciervo?" she whispered in dismay. "If we go closer, he's going to fight even harder." The mud had risen halfway up the colt's side now, and his head, neck, and back jerked and quivered as he fought to break free.

Ciervo answered her by pulling on the reins and stepping toward the colt. Rosa loosened the reins. "You're right, amigo. We need to get closer, even if he is scared," she said. "He won't escape without our help. We're his only chance."

She felt breathless as she rode closer. If only the colt would hold still. His thrashing was making him tip to one side now, and she could hear his panicked breathing, so harsh that it sounded like a whistle. The whites of his eyes glinted in terror from his mud-caked face.

"It's okay, little one," Rosa murmured.

And her words made him struggle even more.

Rosa

A few yards from the mud pit, Rosa slid from Ciervo's back. She dropped the reins to the ground and patted the gelding on the shoulder. "Stay here, amigo," she said, though she knew he didn't need the verbal command. Ciervo was trained to ground tie. A loud snort came from behind her and Rosa spun around to see the stallion posing in front of the mares crowding against the cliff. He snorted again and struck the ground with his front hoof, seemingly ready to take on anyone or anything that dared approach them. Rosa turned back to Ciervo. "Don't worry," she said hopefully and stroked the bay's neck. "I don't think he'll leave his mares."

Slowly she walked toward the colt, the halter and rope in her hand. "It's okay, beautiful boy," she murmured. "I'm not going to hurt you. I promise." She stopped short when the colt erupted into another spasm of terror. "I'm here to help you. Ciervo's going to pull you from the mud. Then you'll be free again. I promise."

The colt stopped struggling and looked at her with wild eyes. "Good boy. That's a good boy," Rosa murmured. She let the rope and halter hang at her side and held her free hand toward him. This time he held still, though his expression was filled with fear-tinged suspicion. She edged closer, and noticed his eyes were a little calmer. Or were they glassier? She moved closer, still murmuring to him.

She couldn't help but appraise him as she advanced. The colt wasn't white, as she'd first thought, but cremello. She could see the blaze running down his face and the pink skin beneath, where he wasn't covered by mud. His head was exceptionally fine, his ears small and nicely shaped, and his eyes large and dark except for their white rim, undeniable evidence of his fear.

She'd noticed the colt before, of course. In fact, he was one of her favorites in the wild herd. She loved his playfulness and love of life. He and the palomino filly always seemed to be running, leaping into the air, or teasing the other horses. The filly was a bit older and bigger, but other than their differences in size and color, they looked remarkably similar. Rosa wouldn't have been surprised to discover they were brother and sister.

"It's okay, boy. Don't worry. I'm here to help you," she continued to speak softly as she drew nearer. The colt strained helplessly against his muddy prison when she reached the edge of the soft ground. She was just a yard away from him now. His breathing was loud, rasping, as he fought to increase the distance between them. "It's okay. Just calm down. Calm down." If only she could communicate that she meant him no harm.

With a loud groan, the colt stopped struggling, and as he relaxed in the mud, he sank even farther. Violent tremors ran through his body and his eyes glazed over.

He's going into shock! Rosa realized suddenly, and dropped to her knees in front of the colt. She waved a hand in front of his face. When he didn't blink, she felt like wailing. Had she come too late to save him? Had he been stuck in the mud for too long? Or was *her* presence the catalyst that had initiated his shock? Was this her fault?

Either way, she had to do something quick. She'd seen a calf go into shock once when she was six years old, and she'd never forgotten it. The poor thing had died, even though its injury hadn't been life threatening. Rosa hadn't understood why even after her father tried to explain it to her, and in a way, she still didn't understand how something could die without a serious injury. But it had happened. She'd seen it with her own eyes. And if she didn't want the same thing to happen to this beautiful two-year-old, she had to act now.

Angelica

She must hurry. Vivo cannot take much more. Should I step forward to help? But what if I go too soon?

It is important that Vivo overcome his fear. If I step forward now, he will not develop the independent trust he needs in this girl – and his life will be altered from the direction it is meant to take.

But if I do not intervene, he may die.

Great One. Please guide me.

Rosa

Rosa reached out to touch the colt's face. He pulled back only a little, then allowed her to rub her fingers over his muddy nose. The mustang was definitely falling into a senseless state. Rosa did not see it as a good sign – but it would allow her to halter him.

With deft movements, she slipped Ciervo's halter onto the cremello head, adjusted it to fit, and backed away, playing out the rope as she went. It reached about three yards from the edge of the softer mud. She noted the distance with a sinking heart. The rope didn't look long enough. In order to pull the colt from the mud, she needed to tie the end around Ciervo's shoulders, loosely enough that he wouldn't choke, and that would take at least a yard of rope. With what was left, the gelding's hind legs would be dangerously close to both the muddy edge and the colt's face.

She looked back at the bay. "Any ideas, amigo?" she asked – and her eyes fastened on the bridle. It was an old bridle, but strong. The leather was thick in both the reins and the headstall. The bit was strong metal. Could she turn the bridle into a harness and tie the rope to that?

But even if it worked, how would she direct Ciervo afterward? How would she convince him to pull? With verbal commands only? Would he understand what she wanted him to do?

I have to try, she decided. *I don't have time to think of another plan.* Rosa dropped the lead rope to the ground and ran to grab Ciervo's reins. She led the gelding toward the pit, then turned him to stand with his back to the colt. "Okay now, amigo," she said, looking into his eyes. "You have to hold still. I know you might not understand what I'm doing, but you can't move until I tell you to, okay?" Ciervo's eyes were locked on the wild horses, standing against the canyon wall. "Listen to me, Ciervo," Rosa insisted and he turned his attention back to her. "Good boy. Now, stay."

Rosa closed her eyes for a moment and let a prayer slip through her mind, then removed the bridle from Ciervo's head. The gelding sniffed at the grass and took a bite. Rosa put her arm under his neck and lifted his head up. "This isn't the time for a snack, amigo," she said. "You have to concentrate. It's important." Busy chewing his mouthful of grass, the gelding eyed her with interest.

Rosa left the bridle hanging upside down against the horse's chest, tied the reins around his neck in a knot and let the ends hang down on either side of his back. She exhaled with relief when she saw the rein ends were long enough to go around Ciervo's girth, barely. The makeshift harness would work. Now if only it was strong enough. With the bit flat against the gelding's chest, Rosa pulled the headstall between his front legs and firmly tied the ends of the reins to the top of the headstall.

"Good boy," she said and stroked Ciervo's neck. "I know you've never been harnessed, amigo, but trust me, it's not scary. It just feels different, that's all."

She went to pick up the end of the lead rope. The colt's eyes were half closed now and his breathing was rapid and shallow. Rosa swallowed the lump that appeared in her throat. Her plan had to work. She couldn't bear it if he died.

She turned back with the rope in her hand, to see that Ciervo had wandered a few steps toward the mustangs. His head was high as he sniffed the air. Then he neighed, a long, powerful cry.

And the stallion answered him! The red herd sire trotted forward, his eyes trained on Ciervo and his gait stiff and high. His tail flowed like a banner behind him. He stopped a few yards from the other mustangs and screamed his challenge. Ciervo half-reared and struck out with a front hoof.

"No!" yelled Rosa. She dropped the lead rope and ran toward the stallion. He didn't seem to notice her. His eyes were locked behind Rosa. He reared and screamed again. And to Rosa's horror, an answering whistle came from behind her. From Ciervo. Had he just accepted the herd sire's challenge?

Angelica

Rojo, come back. You must not fight this one. He will not steal your mares. Ciervo is merely curious, that is all. Please, Rojo, return to your herd.

And Ciervo, I know you can hear me. Please, do what your girl asks of you. Another's life depends on you now. If you do not act quickly, Vivo will not survive.

Rosa

Rosa yelled and waved her arms as she ran. She had to make the stallion leave Ciervo alone, and then somehow calm the gelding and move him back into position without a headstall or halter. It seemed an impossible task.

But she had to try. Otherwise she'd never forgive herself when the colt died – and he *would* die without her help. There was no doubt in her mind. In fact, she might already be too late.

The stallion reared again and pawed the air in front of her, his eyes vivid with rage and fear. Rosa could see the conflict in his expression. His instinct to protect his herd was battling with his fear of humans. And there was something else there too. Another struggle. But what? The stallion's hooves crashed to the ground and he screamed again. Rosa covered her ears with her hands and waited for the answering neigh to blast from behind her. But there was no sound.

Rosa spun around and her mouth dropped open. Ciervo was backing away. And not only that, but he was backing toward the mud pit. "Ciervo?" she whispered, the stallion momentarily forgotten. The gelding stopped in the exact spot Rosa had positioned him earlier and looked at her with bright eyes.

Suddenly Rosa remembered the stallion and turned back to see him walking away from her with a relaxed carriage and smooth gait. What was happening? Why were both horses suddenly backing off? Her presence might have made them stop their fighting, but it wouldn't have made them calm down too. It didn't make any sense.

Could they have decided to put their differences aside until the colt is saved? thought Rosa incredulously. *Horses don't think that way, do they? But what else could it be? Nothing else makes sense.*

She ran back to Ciervo. There was no time to ponder the question. She had to take advantage of the gelding's cooperation. The two-year-old needed to be freed from the mud hole, *now*.

"Okay, amigo," she whispered breathlessly. "Just hold still while I tie his rope to your harness." She used a bowline knot to tie the end of the rope to the knot in the reins at the top of the makeshift harness, and then looked back at the colt. He was in the same position, his eyes closed, his breath shallow and quick.

There's still hope. As long as he's alive, there's hope.

"Come on, Ciervo," she said at the gelding's head. She took hold of his forelock and tugged gently. The bay took a step, then stopped short when the leather tightened around his body. "You can do it, amigo," Rosa encouraged. "I know it feels strange but the ropes won't hurt you. We'll just do this one step at a time, okay?"

She tugged again and Ciervo took another step. Rosa looked back. The rope was taut against the halter, pulling the colt's nose out straight toward the bank. He wasn't struggling against the pressure.

"Keep coming, Ciervo," she said, trying to keep the panic from her voice. "Hurry." The gelding leaned into the rope, and then heaved forward. The leather creaked and Rosa heard a sucking sound. The colt had been pulled a few inches through the mud.

"Good boy, Ciervo! Now a little more." The gelding threw his weight against the leather again and Rosa winced when she saw the reins digging into his shoulders. She glanced back. The colt was almost free. His head was over solid ground now and his body was higher in the mud, closer to shore.

"Just two more steps," Rosa cried. Ciervo leaned against the rope and the colt slid a few more inches from the mud.

Now if only he'd struggle, she thought. *He could reach the bank with his front hooves, if he tried.* She ran back to the two-year-old's head and tugged on his halter. The wild horse didn't respond.

"Again, Ciervo!" she yelled to the gelding and waved him forward. She said another silent prayer that the bridle-harness would hold, that the ancient leathers would be strong enough to withstand the strain. Ciervo groaned as he flung his weight against the traces. His breath was coming in gasps now. With a sinking heart, Rosa realized the leather must be pressing against his windpipe.

But his efforts were paying off. The colt's chest was almost to the bank. She tugged again on the muddy mustang's halter.

"Come on, colt," she yelled in his ear. "You can't give up!" There was a flicker of movement in the colt's eyes – fear.

Good, thought Rosa. *At least that's something! Maybe I can even jar him out of his shock.*

"Stand up! Come on. Stand!" she shrieked as loudly as she could. The colt's eyes sprung open and he jerked back against the rope, then lunged forward, his hooves scrambling for purchase on the soft bank. Rosa threw herself out of the range of his flashing hooves and sprawled clumsily across the dry ground. The colt was acting as if he'd just noticed her.

Ciervo was acting without direction from Rosa now too. As the colt fought for footing, he kept a steady pressure on the rope. His ears were flat against his head as he listened to the colt struggle behind him.

"Good boy, Ciervo," Rosa called out. She jumped to her feet and sent the colt into another frenzy of movement. This time, his hooves caught on solid ground. He dug the hard tips into the earth and groaned as he tried to pull his back legs from the muck. With a loud sucking noise, one of his hind legs came free. And then the other.

And finally, the two-year-old staggered stiff-legged up the bank, his head down and his breath coming in roaring gasps. He was free!

Rosa

The colt stopped a few yards from the mud bank, his head hanging down and his splayed legs quivering. Rosa didn't dare move. He was so close to her. In fact, she would almost touch him if she reached out – but the last thing she wanted to do was send him tumbling into another thoughtless spasm of fear. Then she noticed that his eyes were locked on her, appraising her.

Did he feel too sore and exhausted to move? This could be her chance to unbuckle the halter from his mud-splattered head. She knew it would be far too dangerous to leave it on him. The rope would get tangled on something for sure, and then, unless someone happened along to save him, the colt's end would be even worse than being stuck in a mud pit. He'd waste away slowly from lack of water. But would he let her get close enough to remove it? Somehow she thought he would.

She began speaking in a quiet, soothing voice, telling him he could trust her, that she wouldn't hurt him. Then she told him about her best horse friend, Ciervo, and how they'd met years before. After that, she spoke about her mom and dad, about living on the ranch, and of how much she loved the desert. She even told him that he needed to avoid Senor Garcia or any of his ranch hands other than her father, at all costs. And throughout it all, the colt watched her – and slowly, so slowly, his head came up and his breathing calmed. She wasn't sure when the fear finally left his eyes, but there was a moment, a sudden and magical moment, when she realized he was no longer afraid of her.

"Little horse," she said, her tone filled with wonder. "What's happened to you?" The colt turned to face her and his ears flicked forward. Then he nickered to her. Rosa took a deep breath and cautiously stepped toward him. He stepped away. But she was optimistic. He hadn't tried to gallop back to his herd. He hadn't even pulled on the halter tying him to Ciervo's makeshift harness.

"Are you curious?" she whispered. "Have you ever seen a two-legged creature before?" She stroked Ciervo's cheek as she talked to the cremello colt. "We're pretty funny looking, eh? But we're nice, or at least some of us are. See how Ciervo likes me? He's not scared."

The colt reached out with his nose and his soft muzzle tickled Rosa's arm.

"That's it, little one," Rosa encouraged. "You're so brave. I'm amazed." She raised her hand and he touched her fingers, and then withdrew. Rosa waited and a few seconds later, he sniffed at her again. His nostrils flared gently as he inhaled her scent.

Rosa wondered if she'd ever seen anything so lovely – not just the way the colt looked, but the expression in his eyes. In place of the fear, she could see the light that was his true personality. There was a mischievous glint there, a vivacious curiosity, a lightness of being.

What a terrible thing it would've been if this bright creature had died in the mud pit.

The colt touched her again and without thinking, Rosa moved her fingertips to stroke his nose. "I wish I could take you home with me," she whispered.

Home. I have to get home. If I don't get back in time for supper, I won't be allowed out tomorrow to visit the mustangs!

With slow movements, Rosa reached to unbuckle the halter. The colt rolled his eyes as she tugged gently on the buckle. "It's okay," murmured Rosa. "You want to be free again, I know. Just hold still." She tried once again and the buckle came loose. Slowly she slipped the halter from his head, and then raised her hand to let her fingers linger along his neck. "I'll return as soon as I can, little one," she whispered. "I hope you let me come close to you again."

She felt a sudden lump in her throat. She didn't want to leave him. It made no sense, but somehow she felt she'd known him forever. More than anything, she wanted to take him with her.

Maybe if I gentle him, Senor Garcia will let me keep him on the ranch. But even as she thought of befriending and taming the colt, she realized her hopes were futile. She could never let Senor Garcia know of the two-year-old's existence. The ranch owner hated mustangs, and if he saw the colt, he'd know there were more of them. He'd hunt them down and then send them off to be slaughtered.

She blinked back sudden tears. It wasn't fair. She'd made friends with an amazing mustang, who looked at her with a new and budding trust, and she would only ever be able to spend stolen moments with him.

She turned blindly to Ciervo and worked at loosening the knots in the reins. They were so tight that it took her a few minutes to free Ciervo of his makeshift harness. She was aware of the colt all the while, standing just behind her. She could feel his eyes on her, watching her every movement. She could even hear his soft breath.

When Ciervo was finally ready to go, she turned back. "I'll come back again, little one," she said fervently. "We'll both come back. Tomorrow, if we can. I only hope you'll remember us. That you'll still let us get close to you." Her voice faded away and she felt the tears finally break free and run down her cheek. "Goodbye, my little amigo."

Rosa

"Ciervo, do not leave yet!" The voice rang across the meadow as clear as a bell.

Rosa spun around and the two horses looked toward the herd with heads high. How could a human be there, standing with the mustangs? But the voice *had* come from the wild herd.

She gasped when a willowy girl, about seventeen or eighteen years old, stepped from behind a bay mare.

But they're wild horses, not pets. They shouldn't let a human close to them.

And yet the stallion stood as the girl put an arm around his neck. He trailed after her when she stepped toward Rosa, Ciervo, and the colt. When the others fell in behind, like dogs following their master, Rosa felt the blood drain from her face. This girl was an enchantress, an enchantress of horses!

She glanced at the colt. He was focused on the pale girl walking toward them. Rosa touched the mud-streaked neck and he didn't even notice, confirming the heart-rending thought that had crossed her mind. The enchantress was the one responsible for his gentleness, not her. The only connection between her and this wild colt was in her imagination.

Rosa

The colt neighed to the bright haired girl and trotted toward her. He greeted her with obvious familiarity, and then walked at her shoulder back to Rosa. Ciervo tugged on his reins as the group came near and, still breathless with surprise, Rosa let the leather reins slide through her fingers. The girl greeted Ciervo as if they'd known each other all their lives.

"Hello," she said when they reached Rosa. "My name is Angelica. I have come to thank you for saving Vivo."

"V…Vivo?" Rosa stammered, staring into the girl's strange, golden eyes. "Who's Vivo? Oh. The colt." She blushed and cleared her throat. At least the girl wasn't laughing at her, or so far anyway. She hated how her shyness always made her sound so stupid. If only she could talk to others as easily as Rina. Her older sister was never afraid to talk to anyone about anything. In fact, in Rosa's opinion, she spoke out far too much.

"Yes. His name is Vivo." Angelica answered, her tawny eyes fixed on Rosa's. She smiled. "And he is grateful, as am I. As we all are."

"His name means 'alive'," Rosa whispered, her eyes fixed on the muddy colt. "What a beautiful name." She reached out, intending to rub some of the drying mud from his face, but he shied away. Had she moved too quickly, or didn't he like her anymore?

"It is a lovely name," Angelica agreed. "And because of you, he is *still* alive." She tucked a silken strand of her flaxen hair behind an ear, and then stroked Ciervo's dark neck. "What is your name?" she asked.

"Just Rosa," said the younger girl.

"Just Rosa? I have never heard that name before, Just Rosa."

Rosa felt the heat of embarrassment rise in her face and looked down at the ground. Why hadn't she said *Rosa*? She opened her mouth to explain when the older girl spoke again. "I am sorry. I should not try to be funny. I am not very good at it."

"No, you're fine," said Rosa and looked up at Angelica. The girl was frowning about her unsuccessful joke and the expression didn't seem to fit properly on her face. A hint of a smile touched Rosa's face.

"Really?" Angelica asked, her voice hopeful.

Rosa's smile disappeared. She was even worse at lying. But there was no need to lie – she could see the desire for the truth in Angelica's eyes. Slowly, she shook her head. "No, not really. Sorry. But maybe it wasn't you," she added. "It *was* a terrible joke."

Angelica laughed aloud and her peals of laughter made Rosa smile again. She liked this girl who could laugh at herself, who wasn't embarrassed if she told a bad joke, and who wanted only the truth, even when the truth wasn't what she hoped to hear.

The herd stallion interrupted her musings with a high-pitched neigh and pounded the ground with an iron hoof behind Angelica. Rosa gasped when he pinned his

35

ears back and bared his teeth in Ciervo's direction. She grabbed the gelding's reins and led him away as Angelica turned to face the stallion. At a safe distance, Rosa looked back, just in time to see Angelica place her hands on the red mustang's forehead. She watched, spellbound, as the stallion's head carriage relaxed and his breathing calmed. The fire in his eyes subsided.

No wonder Vivo likes her better than me, Rosa thought reluctantly. *How can I blame him? She truly understands horses. She can even talk to them.*

Angelica lowered her hands and stood silently as the stallion and most of his herd wandered away to graze. Only Vivo and a black filly foal remained at the girl's side. Rosa blinked back unwelcome tears when Vivo nuzzled the golden girl's shoulder. Angelica stroked his neck and he didn't even flinch. The girl scratched the black filly on the forehead with her other hand, then turned her attention back to Rosa.

"Everything is okay now. I told Rojo of Ciervo's intent," said Angelica, speaking softly. "He believed Ciervo wanted to steal his mares, while Ciervo only wanted to become acquainted with the herd members." She looked back at the stallion, grazing beside a gray mare. "I do not blame Rojo for being anxious however," she added. "Many male horses have attempted to steal members of his family, and he is a little sensitive. He especially cannot bear the thought of losing Linda." The gray mare looked up when her name was spoken. "Rojo is torn between two conflicting emotions," Angelica continued. "He knew you and Ciervo were coming to rescue Vivo, but is nervous because both another male horse and a human now know of his family's hiding spot. He feels both gratitude and aggression toward you both. I have reassured him that you mean him no harm."

Rosa suddenly realized her mouth was hanging open, and closed it with a snap. The stallion, who was apparently named Rojo, had told Angelica this? The mare named Linda recognized her own name? And how could Rojo know she was coming to rescue Vivo? Rosa hadn't even known herself. And Ciervo's intent? What did that mean? Everything this girl said was bizarre.

I should be afraid of her, Rosa thought, staring into the amber eyes. She told herself to step back, but even as she did it, she felt there was no need. *I don't feel afraid. Am I like the horses? Am I bewitched by her? Is she using some weird magic on me too?*

"There is nothing to fear from me," said Angelica, echoing her thoughts. "If you have questions about me or something I have done, feel free to ask. I will do my best to explain."

Vivo nickered to Rosa, and she averted her gaze to the two-year-old. The lump in her throat grew larger. There was really only one question she wanted an answer to. "Did you make Vivo be friends with me?" she asked, the words coming out in a rough, cheerless rush.

"No, no," Angelica vehemently replied. "I did not do that. You did. You and Ciervo."

Rosa stared at the ground. She didn't want Angelica to see the doubt in her eyes.

"I mean what I say, Rosa. I did not influence Vivo," Angelica added. Her slender hand touched the younger girl's shoulder. "And you are not Just Rosa. Not to Ciervo nor to me, and certainly not to Vivo. You saved his life."

37

"So you really didn't make him be friends with me?"

"I did *not* make him be friends with you."

"But you could have. I saw what you did to the stallion." With a great effort, Rosa looked up. If Angelica was lying, she hoped to read the falsehood in the luminous eyes. And, like Angelica, she too wanted to see the truth.

"I told Vivo, before you arrived, that someone was coming to save him and I told the others you would not hurt them, and that is all. I did not make him be friends with you. I promise."

A half smile crept onto Rosa's face and she wiped away tears she hadn't even known she'd cried. She believed Angelica. There was an unmistakable honesty to her words and Rosa trusted her, despite her obvious strangeness. That meant that the connection she'd felt between herself and Vivo *had* been real. A feeling of pure joy welled up inside her.

"Approach him yourself," suggested Angelica. "There you will see the final answer to your question."

Rosa collected herself before stepping forward. Vivo looked at her calmly as she approached. She stopped just in front of him. He looked a bit more nervous now, but she could recognize his gentle apprehension for what it was. He was uncomfortable close to her simply because he was unfamiliar with humans, but that didn't mean he didn't want to be friends with her. Slowly she reached to touch his cheek. The hair was silky smooth beneath her fingers. She stroked his unmuddy spots, her eyes on his, and watched the uneasiness gradually leave him.

"Do you see?" Angelica's voice was soft.

Rosa nodded. "He does like me." Vivo nickered and nuzzled her arm. "I wish I didn't have to go," Rosa whispered. "I hope he remembers me." Reluctantly she pulled away from her new friend.

"He will," Angelica promised.

"Thanks, Angelica," Rosa said and took a deep breath. "I thought… well, I thought he only liked me because you told him to."

"No," said Angelica, shaking her head with a smile. "He likes you and trusts you for yourself, and I understand why. You are a very gentle and kind person."

Rosa couldn't think of a response. She cast her eyes down, a shy smile on her face, and turned to Ciervo. "Down, amigo," she said and tapped the top of his neck. Ciervo lowered his head and Rosa leapt to lie across his neck. When the gelding raised his head, she slid onto his back. "I'll bring a brush for you next time, Vivo," Rosa promised once she was astride the bay. The cremello colt snorted.

"I know you must hurry, but before you go I have a gift for you." Angelica held her cupped hands up to Rosa. She dropped her gift into the outstretched palm, and then pulled her hands away to reveal the most beautiful golden chain Rosa had ever seen.

"Angelica, you can't give me this," Rosa protested, all shyness gone. "It must have cost a fortune. I've never seen anything so wonderful." The golden strand tingled in her hand and Rosa felt a sense of well-being flow through her.

"Let me put it around your neck," offered Angelica. "Lean forward."

Rosa shook her head. "I can't, Angelica. Really, it's too good for me. I don't deserve anything like this."

"You saved Vivo's life," said Angelica, putting her hands on her hips. "That is certainly a far better thing than a necklace."

"But..." Rosa stopped. Maybe Angelica was right. Maybe she did deserve something this beautiful. Vivo nickered encouragingly and Rosa took a deep breath. "Okay," she said breathlessly. "And thank you. Thank you so much."

There she goes, Vivo, your gentle Rosa and her dashing Ciervo. What a delightful person she is. No wonder you became devoted to her so quickly.

It seems strange to me, however, that she does not see her own beauty, my friend. I wonder who is really meant to help whom here – is she to help you, as we both supposed? Or are you to help her?

Rosa

As they galloped back across the desert, Rosa was in a fog. She still found it hard to believe she'd made friends with a wild horse! *And in a way, his herd too,* she thought in amazement. *They weren't nearly as frightened of me after I saved Vivo. And, of course, Angelica! There are no words fantastic enough to describe meeting Angelica.*

Rosa touched the necklace at her neck. Its energy thrummed against her fingers and she smiled. Imagine Angelica giving her something so wonderful! The older girl's final words rang through her mind again. "If you need me, just touch the necklace and call my name."

Maybe I should call her tonight, if I can get away for a while after supper. I have to tell her about Bonita. It would be awesome if she could teach me to communicate with horses the way she does.

A sudden thought leapt to the forefront of Rosa's mind and she reined Ciervo to a quick halt. She was so stupid! How could she forget the danger the mustangs were in? Angelica could communicate that to them. It was the perfect opportunity to tell the horses to watch out for the ranch hands, to not leave the canyon unless there was an emergency.

She touched the necklace again and closed her eyes. "Angelica, I need you. Can you hear me?" she whispered hurriedly. "There's something I need to tell you. Something important." The necklace was growing warmer, its energy more distinct. Was it transmitting her message to the enchantress?

But even if Angelica rides one of the mustangs, it'll take her a while to get here, she suddenly realized. *I should've waited to call for her, until I had more time.*

"Rosa? I am here. How may I help you?"

Rosa's eyes popped open and she almost tumbled from Ciervo's back in surprise. Only her other hand, clutching his long mane, saved her from falling. Where had Angelica come from? Was she more than an enchantress of horses? Was she magical?

"I am sorry. I did not mean to startle you."

"Uh, how did you… you didn't ride… you couldn't have so fast… but how else..." Rosa stopped. It was better to say nothing than to babble like an idiot.

"How may I help you?" Angelica asked again. She stroked Ciervo's neck as she waited.

"I need you to tell Vivo and the others something important," Rosa replied, finally catching hold of her reason. "They need to stay hidden in the canyon. Senor Garcia, the ranch owner, doesn't believe wild horses are worth anything. If he sees or hears of them, he'll capture them and ship them off to be slaughtered."

"That is so sad. Does he not know the value of living beings?"

"Some of them, I think," answered Rosa. "The blooded horses. And the ones less than twenty years old." She could hear the bitterness in her own voice.

"But Ciervo…" Angelica stopped speaking and placed pale hands on each side of the gelding's head. A rainbow tear appeared in the corner of each tawny eye.

43

"Ciervo was to be sent away too, but my father stopped it by buying him," Rosa said, anticipating Angelica's question.

The older girl sighed and wiped her tears away. "Three of them," she whispered. "Why did they not call me?"

"What?"

Angelica looked up at Rosa. "Ciervo has already lost three of his best friends this way," she said, her voice trembling with sadness. She paused for a moment to struggle with her emotions. "Did they not understand what was to happen to them? Or were they simply too sad that after a lifetime of service, their owner sent them away to be killed?"

"I'm sorry." Rosa didn't know what else to say. "I wish there was more I could do too." More than anyone, she could understand the helpless despair Angelica seemed to be feeling.

"You should go now, Rosa, before you are too late. I will tell the mustangs to stay in the canyon where they will be safe."

"Thanks," said Rosa. "See you tomorrow." She slipped the necklace down the front of her t-shirt where it would go unnoticed at home, and sent Ciervo on toward the ranch headquarters at a gallop. A few strides from Angelica, an image of Bonita, the sorrel mare her father rode, flashed into her mind – and with it came a bit of hope. Maybe the enchantress could help the mare escape the fate that Senor Garcia had planned for her.

Rosa smiled. She would ask Angelica about saving Bonita tomorrow, when she went to see the mustangs. In the meantime, the older girl was right. She needed to get home. And fast.

My dear Chevy. I hear you calling me. I am coming.

I feel the pain you feel. I feel your agony of spirit. Why is the pain of the heart so much harder to bear than the pain of the body?

Do not worry, my love. I will soon be with you.

Senor Garcia

Senor Garcia walked out onto his private patio. The sun was rising over his empire. His house, built near a small, rocky rise, had views in all directions. He lowered himself to his lounge chair, sipped his steaming coffee, and watched the sunrise glow red before him.

This was his favourite time of day and the time he did his clearest thinking – first thing in the morning, with the entire day stretching into the unknown, its limitless possibilities yet to be discovered. Over the years, he'd learned that a single day could hold much potential, much promise. On each new day, anything was possible.

With his days, he'd accomplished many things, and the view from the patio showed quite a few of them. From where he sat, he could see his corrals and barns, the bunkhouses, and the houses for the ranch hands with families. The sight never failed to make him feel proud and satisfied. He'd done a great deal in this barren place. He'd forced an amazing prosperity from the desert.

Not that it had been easy. It had taken all his discipline, all his energies – and he'd done it alone. The ridicule he'd received from family and friends when he'd first told them he was buying this vast, dry tract of land, still burned in his mind. But he'd proved them wrong, every one of them.

There'd been only one person who'd ever understood him, who'd believed in his vision, and supported him – Liana, his daughter.

He stood abruptly and stalked back inside the house. He'd wasted too much time already, just sitting and thinking. Especially when the thoughts weren't even constructive. There was nothing he could do about Liana. He was powerless to force her back to the ranch. She'd moved beyond his reach.

And there was work to do. The ranch hands would be leaving soon to search for the missing cattle, and this time, he was going with them. It had been a while since he'd been on one of the roundups, too long in fact. It was time he became reacquainted with the farther reaches of his estate. That was a much more valuable use of his time – and far less pathetic – than mooning over a disobedient, runaway daughter.

Angelica

Chevy, my dear, you are safe now. I know it took courage to walk through your cruel owner's yard. We could hear his snores, loud and guttural, as we wove through the debris. I am so grateful he was sleeping deeply. I am grateful, too, that your dog friend, Lizzy, did not bark and rouse him from his slumber.

How cruel this human was to you, Chevy! How vile! The scars and cuts across your back make me shudder in anger. Times like these are the only times I wish I was not bound by non-violence. If I could, I would lock this human in a stall without food, just as he did to you. Then I would keep him there until he was thin and full of despair, as you are, my poor dear. The only thing I would not do is beat him every day, as he did to you. But it is not for me to punish. Only to save, if I can.

Yet I do not understand how he could be so brutal, nor do I see what reward he received from the things he did to you. I do not understand how such unkindness can exist. Oh, Chevy, how I weep for what you have experienced here. Please believe me when I say you did nothing to deserve these brutalities. These abuses were not your fault. The blame lies on the shoulders of your owner alone.

Come now. Let us leave this horrid place that reeks of decay. Let us find some food for you, some fresh, pure water. We must hurry. The sun has risen. We must be gone from here when he wakes and we have far to travel. There is one who waits for you, though he does not know it yet. All creatures need friendship and kindness and this you will give to each other.

Lizzy, come. I cannot leave you here. I know you are loyal to this cruel man. I know you care for him. But if I leave you here, he may punish you beyond your ability to recover. You must say goodbye to him, Lizzy, forever.

Please believe me, there are others who are more deserving of your love.

Rosa

Rosa rolled over in bed and groaned. She felt terrible! Her nose was all stuffed up and her head felt like it was on fire. Groggily, she sat up. Across the room, her older sister was standing in front of the mirror, combing her long black hair. "Rina? What time…" She was suddenly overcome with a fit of sneezing.

"Ew, don't spray in my direction," said Rina. She went to the bedroom door and opened it. "Mama? I think Rosa's sick!"

"I'm fine," said Rosa and swung her feet out of bed. Her face burned as she tried to hold back a coughing fit. Why did she have to get sick today of all days? She had a wonderful wild two-year-old and his herd to become better acquainted with! She grabbed her jeans and pulled them on, then rooted through her drawer for a clean shirt. But she did feel terrible. Her head felt like someone was pounding the inside of her skull with a hammer. And the hot feeling wasn't going away. *Or hasn't gone away yet!* Rosa thought with determination. *I have to get out to Lost Canyon. I want to talk to Angelica some more too. I have so many questions for her.*

Rosa's mother bustled into the room, the thermometer in her hand. "Open up, darling," she said and held the thermometer out.

The desire to cough was becoming almost uncontrollable. Rosa covered her mouth with her hands in an effort to stuff it down. She was unsuccessful. When her mother pulled her hands away, she erupted into violent hacking. Her mother stepped back with a serious look on her face. "Back in bed, young lady," she commanded.

"I knew she was sick," Rina said smugly. "She looks terrible."

Rosa stuck her tongue out at Rina, and then sneezed three times.

"Bless you, my dear. Now you try to get some rest. That's the best thing for a cold," said her mother. "I'll bring you some breakfast. What would you like? Huevos Rancheros?"

Rosa collapsed back against her pillow. Maybe she could rest for just a little while. Then this afternoon she could go out to see Vivo and the herd. "I'm not hungry, Mama," she said. And she wasn't. In fact, she felt like sleeping again, after an entire night of rest.

"I'll bring you something to drink for now," said her mother. She tucked the blankets around Rosa as if she were four years old again. "Are you warm enough, darling?" she asked.

Rosa nodded, her eyes already closing. She'd sleep for just a few minutes. That's all. And by afternoon, she'd feel better, she was sure.

Senor Garcia

Senor Garcia reined in his big black gelding, Macho, at the top of the small rise. The horse stood, muscles tensed and ready for action, as his rider surveyed the wild desert. The other horses stopped beside him and their riders waited for Senor Garcia to speak. "Jose and Manuel check the waterhole."

"Si, Boss."

The two men reined their horses down the sharp incline and cantered away in a trail of dust. Senor Garcia turned to the three still with him. "Carlos, Pedro, Daniel? You go to the foothills. Split up when you get there, and check the whole area by dusk."

"Si, Senor," Carlos agreed. He turned his horse toward the foothills, then reined him in. "Senor, where will you be?" When Senor Garcia frowned at him, he added hastily, "For safety reasons, boss."

"I'm heading to Lost Canyon," said Senor Garcia.

"But if you find them, sir, how will you get them home? What if there are too many?"

"I'll fire my pistol into the air, three times, so you'll know to come." Macho took an impatient step forward. Enough talking, his actions said, and Senor Garcia agreed. He gave the gelding his head and the two slid down the hill and galloped toward the distant canyon.

Angelica

Chevy, Lizzy, we have arrived. This old wooden gate, this overgrown country lane – these lead to your new home. I know it does not look fancy. It even looks a little neglected, but the man who lives here is kind hearted. He will care for you and treat you well. You will have other animal friends here, and best of all, you will have much love, good food, fresh water, and a warm, safe place to sleep at night.

You must go ahead for I cannot let him see me.

I know, Chevy. You are afraid. But this man is kind. You must trust me.

Do not worry. Your past owner will not come for you. He is too afraid the authorities will charge him for his cruelty to you. He will not come forward to claim you or Lizzy. He is too frightened of the law, as he should be, for he was very unkind. You are safe here.

Your new person is a good man. He has given his heart to the animals who live with him – a goat, two cats, another horse, and three dogs. All he rescued from sad situations like yours. He will treat you and Lizzy as his children.

Goodbye, my dear Chevy. Goodbye, my dear Lizzy. I could not leave you in better hands, but remember, if you ever need help again, I am only a call away. Live in peace, my beloved ones, and be well.

Rosa

Rosa woke with a start. She'd been having the most horrible dream. Ciervo was running from malicious people bent on hurting him. Normally, the gelding would be able to outrun any person easily, but these humans had supernatural speed. At first, Rosa had been on Ciervo's back. She'd encouraged him to run faster and faster, but no matter how fast he went, the wicked humans went just a little faster. Then, suddenly, she was up by Rattlesnake Rock, looking at Ciervo and the freaky humans far below. Slowly, slowly, they gained on him until they were almost at his hindquarters, their hands clawing and grasping. And that's when Rosa woke up.

She sat up in bed, breathing heavily. The house was quiet. "Mama? Mama, are you there?" she called out.

There was the sound of movement outside the bedroom and the door swung open. "What do you want?" Rina asked, her voice resentful. Obviously, their mother had told her to take care of her little sister.

"Is Mama here? Or Papa?"

"No, they're at work." Rina started to retreat, pulling the door shut behind her.

"Nothing," said Rosa. "But wait. Where's Papa working today?"

Rina sighed loudly and turned away. "All the men are out looking for the missing cattle. Senor Garcia's in a huff. He even went with them to make sure they searched everywhere." She pulled the door firmly shut behind her.

Senor Garcia went with them? And if they were going to search everywhere, did that mean Lost Canyon too?

Rosa felt her heart was going to stop. She'd told Angelica the horses needed to *stay* in the remote canyon to be safe, but if the men went there, the canyon would become a trap, not a sanctuary.

She groaned and put her head in her hands. She felt dizzy and feverish – but worse than any sickness was the realization she may have put the mustangs in further danger.

Their only chance was if Senor Garcia decided the canyon wasn't worth checking. From what she'd heard, cattle had never been found there before. The ranch owner would know that.

Surely, he wouldn't waste his time, checking a place the cattle never went. Surely, the mustangs would be safe.

Senor Garcia

Senor Garcia directed Macho between the canyon
walls. It felt good to be out, to hear the jingle of spurs,
the squeak of saddle leather, and Macho's hooves
striking stones. He straightened on the gelding's back.
This was exactly what he needed; to get in touch with
the land again. He'd spent far too much time bent over
his desk lately, poring over numbers. Far too much
time hiding from the past.

He winced as Liana filled his mind again. For years,
she'd been the best daughter a man could have – until
the day he discovered she was sneaking out to ride
alone. It was a horrible shock to realize she could ride
a horse better than anyone on the ranch, including
Carlos, the bronc rider; that she wasn't really happy
acting like a proper young lady, and was only
pretending because she didn't want her father to be
upset with her.

When he forbade her to ride without him, to rope or to
spend time helping the ranch hands, the battle began. It
raged for years – until Liana turned twenty and left
him.

He passed an oddly shaped rock with a rocky spur at
the top and looked at it with pained eyes, hardly seeing
it. He'd found the note in her empty room four months

ago and had forced himself to read it, though more than anything he didn't want to know what it said. He read that Liana needed to leave the ranch in order to live her own life, that she didn't want his money but would find her own way in the world – and that she'd been accepted at the University to study to be a veterinarian, a thoroughly unsuitable occupation for a woman in his mind.

As time passed, he waited for her to contact him, thinking it wouldn't be long, but the days stretched into weeks. Then months. To stop himself from phoning the telephone number she'd scrawled at the bottom of her note, he crumpled the paper and shoved it in the back of his file cabinet. If he called her, he would be letting her win! And he hadn't done anything he needed to apologize for. He'd only been trying to protect her.

Macho snorted and half reared, bringing Senor Garcia's thoughts back to the present. The meadow stretched out before them, ringed by impassable stone walls. And it was occupied. The black horse pawed the ground in excitement. The man too, felt a thrill course through him.

Mustangs! On his ranch!

Vivo. Greetings to you and the herd. Did you have a good night's rest?

I am sorry I could not come sooner. I have a message for you from Rosa. She says you must stay in this canyon and hide. You must not venture forth for some time. The man who owns this land does not like mustangs and you must avoid...

Wait!

Someone is there! Someone is watching us! One of the ranch hands?

Has the danger Rosa warned us of found us anyway?

Senor Garcia

Senor Garcia scowled. No wonder the cattle were gone. They'd probably broken through the fence somewhere, looking for food, because these nags, these vermin, had eaten their grass.

He pulled his pistol from the holster and fired it three times into the air. The ranch hands wouldn't arrive for a while, but the mustangs weren't going anywhere. He could wait.

The herd stallion left his group and paced a short distance toward the man and horse. Macho trembled and the man tightened the reins.

"Quiet now," he said. "No reason to get all nervous. That's not even a horse, not a real one. It's a pest. And it's up to us to get rid of it."

Suddenly the stallion wheeled about. Senor Garcia gasped. In flight, the red horse looked magnificent. He nipped his herd into a run and they streamed toward the back of the meadow like a multi-colored wave.

In the middle of the wave, a golden crest glittered in the sun. Senor Garcia blinked. What was that? One of the mustang's tails? It had to be.

I must go, my beauties!

Please, I am not abandoning you, but I cannot attempt to save you here. The risk to you is too high. The man who blocks our escape has a gun that he may use on you. And even if we all successfully stampede past this man, others are coming. He signalled to them by firing his gun into the air and they will be rushing toward us at this very moment.

But be ready to act, be ready to run, when I come again.

Rosa

Rosa's eyes opened wide. She'd fallen asleep again! She started to sit up, then fell back on her pillow and squeezed her eyes shut. Her head felt like it was splitting open! She took a deep breath in and held it in for a moment, hoping the pain would pass. It didn't.

"Rina? Mama? Is anyone there?"

No response.

Rosa groaned. She needed some pills to help relieve the pain. And a huge glass of water. She was *so* thirsty.

"Rina?" she tried, one more time.

Silence. Rosa forced herself to sit up and swing her legs over the edge of her bed. She'd have to get her own medicine and water. She shut her eyes again when the room spun around her, and breathed as calmly and steadily as possible until the dizziness passed. How she hated being sick!

She shuffled through to the kitchen. It was deserted. Rosa looked at the clock above the stove. It was late afternoon. Her mother would be home soon from Senor Garcia's house, where she did the cooking and cleaning. And her father? He could be back anytime, but on this day, later was better as far as Rosa was concerned. If the men found the wild horses, they'd herd them back to the ranch headquarters right away, and therefore every minute that passed without them showing up was a sign the mustangs hadn't been found.

She grabbed the bottle and took out two pills, then gulped them down with a glass of water. A couple minutes later, she was back in bed and fast asleep.

Senor Garcia

Senor Garcia was surprised – he was actually enjoying watching the mustangs. After he and Macho had stood silently for a few minutes, the two foals, a black and a chestnut, started playing together. At first, their dams whinnied to them nervously, but when the man and his horse didn't make any aggressive moves, they relaxed. Then a young palomino started to graze against the far wall, her golden coat glistening in the sunlight. Moments later, a muddy colt joined her.

It was no wonder they felt safe. The stallion, a well-muscled, rugged beast, was standing between them and the threat. Every few minutes, he'd send a challenge to Macho, and Senor Garcia had to tighten the black's reins to remind him not to respond.

As he waited for help to arrive, Senor Garcia cast an appraising eye over the herd. There wasn't even one he'd consider keeping. They were too small and coarse, not one bit like the tall, elegant blooded stock he kept for his ranch horses. Now those were horses a man could be proud to own.

Some of the mustangs might make good kid's horses – they were certainly small enough – but he wasn't in the business of breaking horses for kids. He'd have to ship them to the slaughterer. Maybe the money he'd get would pay for the grass they'd stolen from him and his cattle, if he was lucky.

Suddenly the mustangs' heads shot up and the foals rushed back to their dam's sides. A second later, Senor Garcia heard hoofbeats clattering up behind him. Carlos, Pedro, and Daniel had arrived. It was time to get down to business.

Rosa

Rosa woke briefly when her mother came home from work and tried to get her to swallow some broth. She managed a few spoonfuls, took some more medicine, and fell back into a restless sleep, full of dreams.

She dreamed of clinging to Ciervo's mane as he flew across the desert. The cremello colt galloped behind him, struggling to keep up. And behind him, Rojo, Linda, and the others followed, their eyes rolling back to see something behind them. Something that Rosa couldn't see, no matter how many times she tried. Something that terrified them. Their hoof beats saturated her dreams like thunder.

Half aware, she felt her mother touch her forehead with her cool hand. "Mama?"

"Hush, darling. Just rest. Rest."

Rosa didn't bother opening her eyes. "I was dreaming of mustangs."

"Go back to sleep, Rosa. It's night time now."

She heard her mother's soft footfalls as she walked away, and the creaking of springs as her older sister turned over on her bed. Then the sounds turned to hoofbeats and she was off again, racing over the desert.

Senor Garcia

Senor Garcia picked up the phone and dialled.

"Sorry to bother you so late, Senor Domingo. This is Senor Garcia. How are you?"

A short silence as he listened to Senor Domingo's response.

"Ah, that's too bad. I hope your son sees his folly soon, Senor Domingo."

Another silence, longer this time. Senor Garcia tapped his fingers on his desk as he waited for Senor Domingo to finish complaining about his son. He hated this small talk, especially with Senor Domingo. And what did the man have to complain about anyway? At least his son was talking to him. At least his son hadn't shut his father out of his life.

"Si, si. I do have a bunch for you," Senor Garcia said quickly, when the slaughterer turned the conversation back to business. "Twelve mustangs and an old ranch horse. Can you come tomorrow?"

There was another long pause as Senor Domingo checked his schedule. Senor Garcia suspected the man was taking longer than was necessary, in an effort to accentuate his own importance to the rich landowner. Finally, he came back on the line.

"Two o'clock tomorrow it is, then," Senor Garcia agreed, and hung up the phone before the slaughterer could say anything more.

Quickly, he readied himself for bed. He was tired. It had been a full day, and though they hadn't yet found the missing cattle, it had been an oddly satisfying day.

But when he got into bed, he couldn't sleep. He tossed and turned for hours, staring into the darkness. Finally, in the small hours of the morning, he slept – and dreamt of Ciervo, the horse he'd sold to Jose for his daughters. The horse's mane and tail shone ebony in the sun and rainbow light rippled over his slick body. The man was enjoying the dream until Jose's daughter appeared. She stood beside Ciervo and pointed directly at him, and he knew she was accusing him. But of what? He hadn't done anything wrong.

Then suddenly, she wasn't Jose's daughter any longer. She was Liana. With his heart in his throat, he watched her open her mouth to tell him something. Was she coming home? Was she finally admitting that he was right? He leaned forward, eager to hear what she had to say – and the mustang stallion's challenge sounded from her throat!

Angelica

I am here to set you free, Rojo. Be silent now. Let us not arouse attention.

The gate is chained shut. Locked. It will take a few moments to unfasten. Patience, my friends. Patience.

Senor Garcia

Senor Garcia sat bolt upright in bed, his eyes wildly searching the darkness, his breath ragged and panicky. The stallion's cry seemed to pull from the dream and linger in the night.

But that's impossible! It's just a dream. It's not real! But then he remembered – the mustangs were outside, in one of the corrals. The stallion must be expressing his rage at being locked up. That was what turned the dream into a nightmare. It had nothing to do with the girl or Liana. There was nothing they could accuse him of.

He lay there for a few more moments, and then rose from his bed. He wouldn't go back to sleep now anyway.

The moon streamed down onto the milling horses as he walked across the ranch yard. Everyone was asleep, except the horses. The ones he had condemned to die would be his only companions this night.

Moonlight highlighted sudden movement by the gate. Something was there, something much too small to be a horse! Or was it someone – someone who wanted to free the mustangs!

With a bellow, he rushed forward. The intruder ran off into the shadows, almost impossibly swift. When he *reached the gate, Senor Garcia took the lock and chain in his hand. The lock felt warm but was still intact.*

He'd been right then, to lock the corral. The disapproval he'd seen in some of his employees' faces as they'd herded the mustangs back to the ranch had been real. Someone on the ranch thought the mustangs should be freed; either one of the ranch hands, or possibly one of their family members.

Like Jose's youngest daughter, the one he'd dreamed of. The one who'd pointed at him. Accused him.

Was that why he'd dreamed of her?

Rosa

Rosa woke and stretched. She drew in a deep breath. She felt so much better. Her headache was gone; her fever was gone. It must have been a twenty-four hour flu that had run its course. She was cured, and starving!

She swung her legs out of bed. No dizziness. So far, so good. Then she was standing. "I feel great!" she enthused to her sister.

Rina groaned in response and put her hand to her forehead. "I feel terrible," she mumbled.

"Mama," called Rosa, "I think Rina's sick."

"Quiet," whimpered Rina. "My head's splitting."

"Sorry," murmured Rosa. And she meant it. She knew *exactly* how terrible Rina was feeling. "I'll get Mama," she offered. "And I'll bring you some water. You'll feel thirsty soon."

"Thanks." Rina's reply was almost inaudible.

Rosa walked out to the kitchen. No one was there. She glanced at the clock above the stove. No wonder. She'd slept in. Both her father and mother had already left for work and she remembered something about Rina going to a friend's house to spend the night.

She poured a large glass of water for Rina, removed two pills from the bottle, and carried them into the bedroom. Rina looked as if she was sleeping again, and Rosa was careful to be quiet. The more her older sister could sleep through her flu attack, the better. She put the glass down on the bedside table, crept from the room, and gently pulled the door shut behind her.

Rosa wandered to her desk at the living room window and picked up her big math textbook. If she could get enough schoolwork done this morning, maybe her mother would let her out to ride that afternoon, even though she'd been sick the day before. It was worth a shot. She ached to see Vivo again, and besides, she wanted to know for sure that the horses were still safe.

They hadn't been brought to the ranch, she was sure of that. She was relieved she'd guessed right – the ranch hands probably hadn't wasted their time checking the canyon. She'd have heard the mustangs gallop past their house on their way to the corrals, and besides, her parents would have said something. But still, she'd feel better when she saw them safe in Lost Canyon with her own eyes.

Her gaze caught movement and she looked through the window above her desk to see Carlos, one of the men her dad worked with, striding past the house. Why wasn't he out rounding up the missing cattle? Had they found them all already? Slowly, the math book sunk back to the desk and she rose to her feet. She could see dust hanging over the corrals. Something was in there. And because of what Carlos was carrying, she didn't think it was cattle.

The dizziness came back in a rush and Rosa clutched the edge of her desk to hold herself steady. Carlos held his coiled lariat in one hand. That wasn't unusual. What was abnormal was the thick leather headstall and heavy rope gripped in his other hand – his bronc riding gear.

There were no bucking horses on the ranch, only well-mannered saddle horses, and the only time Senor Garcia used Carlos' talent as a bronc rider was when they caught wild horses. The ranch owner was a smart businessman. He knew he'd get more money for a good bucking horse than he would from the slaughterer, so he always had Carlos ride them, one by one, to see if they were good enough buckers to sell to the rodeo.

But I would have heard them gallop past the house. It can't be them!

And suddenly she remembered her dreams, and the hoofbeats like thunder. She *had* heard the horses gallop past. She *had* heard them milling about in the corral. And she'd incorporated the sound into her dreams.

Now her only chance to free them was gone. She could have snuck out to free them last night if she'd realized the sounds were real. The mustangs could now be safe and sound, miles from the ranch buildings if she hadn't slept so heavily, if she hadn't gotten sick! This was all her fault.

Senor Garcia

Senor Garcia nodded to Carlos when the bandy-legged bronco rider joined him at the fence. "They don't look like much, do they, Carlos?" he said.

The smaller man didn't respond for a moment, and when he finally spoke, his voice was soft. "They ain't that bad, boss."

Senor Garcia looked down, his eyes questioning.

"You're used to the blue-bloods," Carlos continued. "The thoroughbreds, the Spanish horses. These ain't that, that's for sure, but they're strong and tough, they're sound and they're smart too. They'd make better... uh, good ranch horses, you know?"

Senor Garcia appraised the herd again. Could Carlos be right? He trusted the horse wrangler's opinion on most things. Was he spoiled in having the money to buy aristocratic horses? And what was Carlos going to say before he changed the tack of his sentence? That this motley herd would make better ranch horses? Better working horses?

The pale two-year-old raised his head and Senor Garcia noticed the colt wasn't white, as he'd first thought, but a cremello. The young horse stepped toward them, his ears forward. Behind him, a gray *mare nickered quietly, her eyes watching them with interest.*

"I could, uh, break them out for you," Carlos suggested quietly. "Then you'd see for yourself how good they'd be."

Senor Garcia inhaled sharply. Now he understood. Carlos didn't want the mustangs sent to the slaughterhouse. He was trying to save them with a lie to his boss. Could Carlos be the one who'd tried to free the mustangs last night?

"No," he said brusquely. "Just see if there are any good broncs among them. I already phoned Domingo. He'll be here at two, so be finished before then."

"You can't do that." The quiet voice came from behind them and both Carlos and Senor Garcia looked around to see Jose Fernandez's daughter staring at them with accusing eyes. Senor Garcia almost expected her to raise her hand and point at him as she'd done in his dream, but she didn't. Instead, she spun away and raced back toward her house.

Only Carlos watched her go.

Rosa

Rosa ran toward her house, but when she reached it, she didn't stop on the tiny veranda or go into the comforting kitchen. She continued to run, hardly recognizing where she was going.

Senor Garcia had already phoned for the slaughterer and he was to arrive at two o'clock! Her heart felt it was going to burst with grief. And what made everything even worse was the mustangs trusted her now. Vivo had stepped toward her as she'd approached the corral behind Senor Garcia and Carlos. Linda had whinnied to her for help.

But what could she do? Carlos would be with the horses, throwing them down to saddle them, and then riding them, one by one, for the next few hours. And Senor Domingo was going to be there at two.

Rosa came to a stop near the big ranch house, breathing heavily from her run. It was a long shot, but maybe her mother could do something. She checked to make sure the necklace was still hidden beneath her t-shirt, then raced around the house to the side entrance, the one her mother used when she went to work. Rosa pounded on the door and footsteps sounded on the ceramic tile floor on the other side of the heavy wood.

"Mama!" Rosa launched herself forward and wrapped her arms around her mother's waist when the door opened. "You have to help!"

"What is it, Rosa? Is it Rina? Is she okay?" She was already untying her apron.

"She's all right," said Rosa, pulling away. "She's sleeping. This is worse, Mama. Much, much worse!"

"Come inside and have a cup of hot chocolate. I think I know what you're going to say." She retied her apron as she walked back to the stove.

Rosa followed her mother into the huge kitchen and sat at the long wooden table. Delicious smells wafted around her and her stomach complained, loudly and suddenly. "You know about the wild horses?" she asked, though she'd already guessed the answer. Of course, her mother knew. She would've known last night, when the mustangs were herded into the corrals.

"Si, the mustangs. I wondered if you'd discover they were here." She poured milk into a pot to heat as she spoke.

"Why didn't you tell me?"

"You know how you get when Senor Garcia brings in the wild ones. The last time you cried for days. We were hoping you wouldn't notice." Her mother put a warm cinnamon pastry in front of Rosa and sat across the table from her. Her eyes searched her daughter's face. "And we're already trying to help them. Your father had to go out looking for the missing cattle today, but he knew Carlos would stay to ride the mustangs. He asked him to talk to Senor Garcia about turning them into ranch horses, so there is still a chance."

Rosa shook her head. Emotion welled up inside her, closing off her voice and forcing tears from her eyes. At least her parents and Carlos had tried. But she'd overheard the conversation with Senor Garcia. Their efforts had been fruitless.

"What's wrong, darling?"

With a voice ravaged by sadness, Rosa told her. Her mother sighed again and rose to her feet. She spooned cocoa into the milk and stirred, deep in thought. Finally, she walked back to the table, two full cups in her hands. She put one cup in front of Rosa and sat down with a heavy sigh. "You know there is nothing more we can do, don't you, Rosa? If we become forceful, Senor Garcia will only fire us, and we'll be forced to leave the ranch."

Rosa nodded mutely. She didn't want to leave the ranch any more than her parents did. It had been their home for as long as she could remember. But she couldn't let the mustangs be shipped off to a horrible, frightening death either. She lifted the cup of cocoa and blew on its steaming surface, her mind in a fog. What could she do? All she could think of was how few options she had, how little power.

Yet there had to be a way.

"Rosa, what are you thinking? You won't do anything silly, will you?"

"No, nothing silly," Rosa answered truthfully. It wasn't silly to try to save lives. Her mother and father might not be able to act against Senor Garcia, but she could, as long as she did it without her parents' knowledge. Then, if she were caught, she could honestly say they knew nothing of her plans. That should save their jobs, or so she hoped.

"Thanks, Mama, for trying to save them." She put the untasted hot chocolate back on the table and stared at the cold pastry lying in front of her. "I'm going to try to get some homework done. Maybe it'll help me forget," she added as she stood.

"I'm sorry, Rosa," her mother said. "I wish we could do more."

"Me too," Rosa whispered from the doorway.

"I'll see you at lunchtime, darling."

"Bye, Mama." Rosa slipped from the big house and closed the door firmly behind her. She appreciated her parents' efforts and understood their position. But she wasn't duty-bound as they were. She would try to free the mustangs.

But how? She needed a plan. And quickly.

Rosa

The answer came when she was halfway back to the corral. A sudden hot breeze blew a free strand of her dark hair across her face, and when she pushed it back, her hand accidentally brushed against the necklace. Maybe she didn't have to think of a brilliant plan. She could summon Angelica. Why hadn't she thought of it before? The enchantress might know how to free the mustangs.

But she couldn't summon Angelica right here. She'd have to go somewhere safe from prying eyes. Rosa ran toward the big barn. Hopefully, her father hadn't turned Ciervo out to pasture, thinking she'd be too sick to ride him for a few days. Vivo whinnied to her as she ran past the corrals to the barn, but Rosa didn't stop. If she wanted to save him, she had to hurry.

"Ciervo!" she called when she stepped into the shadowy interior. A chorus of neighs greeted her. There were four horses inside today, Senor Garcia's Macho, Ciervo, Carlos' big saddle horse, and Bonita. Rosa stopped short. Had her father come home early? She hurried to the sorrel mare's stall. There was no evidence of dried sweat on her shoulders, no sign that she'd been out that morning. So why wasn't her father riding her?

80

The logical answer came in a flash. Bonita was to be sent off with the mustangs today! Senor Garcia was sending her off earlier than expected, so he wouldn't have to pay Senor Domingo to make two trips.

She slipped inside the stall and threw her arms around the mare's neck. "Oh Bonita, how can he be so cruel? I'll do my best to save you too. I promise." The mare sighed contentedly and nuzzled Rosa's shoulder.

To her, this is just a day off, the girl realized. *She doesn't know what Senor Garcia's done or what's going to happen to her. She has no idea why I'm so upset.*

She pulled away and ran her fingers through the silky forelock. "It's probably better if you don't know," she whispered and laid her cheek against the mare's starred forehead. "But remember, if anything scary happens, if you don't understand what's going on, just know that I'm doing my best to save you all."

Rosa

Moments later, Rosa was in Ciervo's stall. She haltered the gelding, then slipped the bit into his mouth and the headstall over his ears and, using the mounting block, jumped onto his bare back. Ciervo's ears pricked toward the mustangs as he and Rosa left the barn, then he neighed loudly. Rojo answered immediately and trotted to meet him. The stallion stopped in the middle of the large corral and snorted, then bellowed a challenge. Rosa couldn't help but smile, just a little. "He's still worried you're going to steal his lovely Linda," she whispered to the old gelding.

A rope snaked out from the edge of the corral and settled around the stallion's neck. Rojo squealed in frustration and ducked his head, but he was too late. The noose was tightening. He was caught.

Rosa felt the smile slide from her face. She spun Ciervo away and urged him into a gallop. She couldn't bear to watch Carlos ride the wild horse. He wouldn't be taking his time, as he did while training the young ranch horses. Instead, he'd snub Rojo down, forcefully saddle and bridle him, then climb onto his back and encourage him to buck.

But he has no choice either, she thought. *Carlos is only doing what Senor Garcia expects him to do.*

Within minutes, they'd arrived at their destination: a small grove of trees near an artesian spring. The desert animals went there to drink, but the men rarely visited the spring except to water their saddle horses, and because the spring was so close to the ranch buildings, they rarely did even that. It would be a safe, quiet place to call Angelica.

She rode Ciervo along the trail beside the spring, and slipped from his back beside the still pool of water. The gelding stepped forward to drink and Rosa settled on the grass. She closed her eyes and touched the necklace. "Angelica," she whispered. "Can you hear me? We need you. The mustangs and Bonita need you."

She gasped as she felt an immediate sapping of her energy and put a hand on the grass to stop from sagging toward the ground. This hadn't happened last time! Was the necklace running out of energy?

A sudden sharp tugging at her heart made her cry out, and she felt as if part of herself was being jerked far away. An image sprung into her mind, an image of impossibly green fields and a roan mare licking a newborn foal, dark with wetness. Angelica was standing beside the mare and she looked up suddenly, as if she'd heard Rosa's cry. Then as suddenly as it came, the image vanished.

Rosa heard water drops falling from Ciervo's lips and the gelding moving back to stand beside her. She heard a tiny wind sigh as it slipped through the leaves on the trees. And she heard a soft step.

"Rosa?"

Her eyes opened. It had worked again. Angelica was standing in front of her. "It's the wild horses," she blurted out and climbed weakly to her feet. "They've been captured and the horse slaughterer is coming. And he'll be taking Bonita too. He'll be here at two and we have to save them before then or it'll be too late!"

"Oh no. I hoped we would have more time."

"So you knew they were captured?"

Angelica nodded. "Yes. I tried to free them last night, but Macho's man came along just in time to stop me. Then he stayed to guard the mustangs until first light." A pensive look crossed her face. "We must act soon. Will they be unattended anytime before the slaughterer arrives?"

Rosa shook her head. "Carlos is riding them right now. Senor Garcia wants to see if he can sell any of them as broncs to the rodeo."

Angelica frowned. "Do you think this Carlos will stop for lunch?"

"I don't know." Rosa shrugged. "He might, if he's ridden most of them by then."

"Then there is our opportunity to save them. We will ensure the riding will be finished by then."

"How?"

"I will ask the horses to cooperate with Carlos. I will ask them to not attempt to buck him off."

Rosa

Rosa was so surprised by Angelica's statement that she laughed aloud – and instantly felt bad. Obviously, Angelica could communicate with horses and who was she to doubt the older girl? "Sorry," she said, meekly.

"I am not angry," said Angelica with a comforting smile. "Now let us go to where we can keep watch over the horses. Is there a vantage point where we can see them, yet will not be noticed ourselves?"

Rosa thought for a moment. "Si, I can think of one place, but we'll have to leave Ciervo here. Most of the path is too steep for him." They left the gelding in the grove and headed back along the trail, then began climbing up the rocky hillside. About a third of the way up the incline, Rosa stopped to catch her breath. Though her energy was returning, she was still tiring too easily after her experience with the necklace. "When we get to the top, we'll be able to see the ranch buildings and corrals," she gasped. "They'll see us too, if we don't stay low."

"I will stay down," said Angelica, her breath unhurried. She seemed unaffected by the climb.

Rosa nodded and continued. The slope was getting steeper and rockier, and the sun beat down on them mercilessly. After a couple minutes, she had to stop again. "A couple years ago, Senor Garcia caught some mustangs, Angelica. Nine of them. Why didn't you help them?" She leaned into the shadow of an overhang and wiped the sweat from her forehead with the back of her hand.

Angelica stopped below her and her brilliant hair shimmered as she shook her head. "I did not know they were in danger, Rosa. They did not call me. Most mustangs are very independent and strong-minded. They may have believed they would find some way to escape. Mustangs do not understand the ways of humans, and they have no idea that places of slaughter exist. Such things are unimaginable to them." She shuddered.

It took only a few more minutes to climb to the top of the rise. They walked, doubled over, to the edge of the hill on the other side and lay down so as not to be seen from below. The ranch buildings spread out beneath them, orderly and neat. Rosa pointed to the corrals.

Carlos had snubbed Rojo to the center post in a smaller corral. The saddle was already cinched around the powerful girth and the stallion stood with all four legs braced against the rope around his neck. His ears were pinned back and he looked at Carlos with half-frightened, half-furious eyes.

Suddenly, he leapt into the air in an explosion of movement. He jerked back against the rope, and then ran forward in the other direction. He hit the end of the rope with a snap. His head jerked around and he flipped onto his side.

Carlos was on top of the stallion in less than a second, his knee heavy on the horse's muscular neck, pinning his head to the ground. Rojo thrashed and squealed in his efforts to stand, but with the man on his neck, he was helpless.

"Carlos isn't a bad person," said Rosa, afraid that Angelica would think he was being horribly cruel. She knew how much the small man loved horses, and how many horses on the ranch loved him. They trusted him because he was kind and fair. "Senor Garcia said he had to ride all of them today, so he's forced to go way too fast."

Angelica nodded, her face pained. Then her eyes squeezed shut in concentration. Rosa looked back to the struggling stallion and the man. The first thing she noticed was that Carlos seemed to relax. He started to stroke the red horse and then, in a single swift motion, was off Rojo's neck. But the stallion didn't leap up immediately. He lay still for a few moments, then raised his head, looked around, and calmly stood. He shook the dust from his body and turned to gaze at Carlos, his ears pricked forward. The horse wrangler walked forward to brush more of the dust from the stallion's coat with his hand.

"Wow," whispered Rosa, when he started scratching Rojo beneath his mane. The horse stretched his neck out so Carlos could reach a bit more. "It's like magic." She looked at Angelica with awe. "How did you do that?"

Angelica laughed softly beside her. "It is not really magic," she said. "You have seen I have a gift for communicating with horses, but sometimes other animals understand me as well. I told Rojo to save his energy, as well as let him know the man would not hurt him, even though some of the things he would do might seem strange. Carlos sensed my communication and became calmer himself. I think he must be half-horse to have understood so easily." She smiled.

"You should try your communication thing on Senor Garcia."

"Hmmm. Now that might be a good idea," Angelica said beside her. "Between the two of us, we may just convince him to set them free."

Senor Garcia

Senor Garcia straightened in his chair and stretched. He'd been hunched over his desk all morning and needed some fresh air. His face creased in pain as he stood and his body protested to the change in position. He leaned on his desk for a moment and let his back stretch out. He'd definitely been sitting for too long. He needed to do a bit of walking. He wanted to see how Carlos was doing anyway. The horse wrangler should be almost halfway through the herd by now.

The ranch owner walked from the house and immediately starting perspiring. It was a hot day for sure! He turned the corner of the big house to see Carlos sitting on one of the mustangs, a pinto mare – and she wasn't fighting him.

A puzzled look crept onto Senor Garcia's face. The horse couldn't already be trained to ride, could it? But what else would explain her calm, unpanicky demeanor? Could she be an escapee from one of the neighboring ranches?

He leaned on the fence and watched Carlos dismount. The bronc rider uncinched the saddle and slid it from the horse's back, then removed the headstall. The mare wheeled away and trotted toward the mustangs pressing against the far side of the fence in a neighboring corral. Carlos followed her to open the corral gate, hazed her inside to join the others, and walked toward his boss.

"I wonder whose horse that is?" asked Senor Garcia. "She sure looks like a mustang."

"I'm sure she is, boss," Carlos said slowly, sounding as if he were choosing his words carefully. "It's the strangest thing. They've all been like that, calm and relaxed, except the stallion right at first. But when I get on them, they don't know anything. A broke horse would know how to rein and stop and back, but they don't know how to do anything at all. They're just very intelligent, sensible, and willing to learn."

Senor Garcia was speechless. He'd never heard of such a thing before. A wild horse that would allow itself to be ridden, that wasn't afraid?

"There's one left to ride," Carlos said. "She'll probably be like the others. You want to watch? It won't take long."

"Sure." Maybe if he watched from the sidelines, he'd see something that Carlos had missed, something that explained the strange phenomenon.

Carlos opened the gate where the mustangs had first been held and the last mustang, a small bay mare, trotted into the main corral. With the headstall in one hand and the other held out to the mare, Carlos walked toward the mustang. She stood firm and allowed him to touch her head and neck without shying away. Expertly, he slipped the hackamore over her nose, the headstall over her ears, and tugged lightly on the rope reins. The mare lifted her head at the pressure, but didn't step forward. Obviously, she didn't know he wanted her to follow him.

Carlos patted her on the neck, then walked to her left and pulled gently on the rope. Her head came around and he praised her as he stroked her neck. He walked to her right side, and this time when he put pressure on the rope, she stepped cautiously toward him. He praised her again, and then moved back to her left. She stepped after him without hesitation this time.

"Now look at this," he said to his boss and walked directly away from the mare, the reins in his hand. Senor Garcia's mouth dropped open when the mustang followed Carlos, her ears pricked forward and her eyes calm. Carlos had just taught her to lead!

The wrangler led the mare to the saddle and saddle pad, let her sniff at them, and then saddled her. Though the mustang rolled her eyes in apprehension, she didn't move the entire time Carlos tacked her up. Finally, he put one foot in the stirrup and, in one graceful motion, was on her back. The mare stood completely still, her ears back, listening to him.

"So what do you think, boss?"

"I've never seen anything like it."

"It would be easy to train them all and use them for ranch horses," Carlos suggested again, a trace of new hope in his voice. A frown flashed onto Senor Garcia's face and Carlos looked down, his face suddenly weary. He patted the mare on her neck and dismounted, then started to unsaddle her.

Senor Garcia watched him loosen the leathers and remove the saddle. The horse wrangler obviously didn't want the horses sent to slaughter. But to what lengths would Carlos go to save them? Would he drug the mustangs to make them appear gentler than they really were, in an effort to convince his employer to keep them? If only he had proof that Carlos was the one who'd tried to free them last night. If he were capable of that, wouldn't he easily justify doing something as dishonest as drugging them too?

Mr. Garcia had always thought Carlos was an honest man, yet now, for the first time, he wondered. His thoughts pained him. He hated it when someone he trusted betrayed his trust. And for what? Some mangy, worthless mustangs! But maybe Carlos was innocent too.

If I don't do what he asks, I'll never know whether he's guilty or innocent, Senor Garcia realized with a start. I won't see the mustangs again after Senor Domingo takes them, and so I'll never know if they're drugged or not. I'll have to keep one or two, and see if they start acting like normal mustangs in a little while, after the drugs wear off.

Senor Garcia watched his employee remove the headstall and the mare trot toward the others, her head high. The red stallion greeted her with a piercing neigh. With hackamore in hand, the wrangler turned back to Senor Garcia, his eyes flat with hopelessness.

"It's too late to cancel with Senor Domingo now and he'll be upset if he comes all this way for nothing," said Senor Garcia. "But you can select two of the twelve to work with. Senor Domingo can take the rest."

A surprised smile flashed onto Carlos' tanned face. "Thanks, boss," he said – and his voice was grateful, his gaze seemed genuine, his smile truthful.

"No, keep four," said Senor Garcia, suddenly feeling generous. If Carlos was innocent, he deserved to be rewarded anyway. He'd always been a good, reliable worker, and he'd done a fantastic job with the *mustangs. "The four best ones," he added. "But not the stallion or any young ones."*

"Thanks, boss," repeated Carlos. "You won't regret it. They ain't as pretty as your blooded stock, but they'll be tough and smart. Good in the hills."

Senor Garcia nodded. "I hope so," he said and smiled tentatively at his hired hand. "I hope so."

Rosa

Their plan was in place, but Rosa didn't know how she was going to summon the courage to do her part. She twisted her braid as she thought of standing in front of Senor Garcia, her heart thudding in her ears, trying to form words. How was she going to convince the ranch owner to let the mustangs go, even with Angelica's weird thought messages trying to influence him? And the second part of their plan seemed even more impossible, convincing him to let the horses return to Lost Canyon! How was she to do that?

But that would be the perfect solution. If the ranch owner let the mustangs return to Lost Canyon, if that could become their designated area on the ranch, she'd see them again. She'd get to spend time with Vivo and the others. But most important of all, the mustangs would have a permanent home, safe from the neighbouring ranchers as well. It would be the ideal situation, *if* they could convince Senor Garcia.

She watched with apprehension from their vantage point as Carlos dismounted from the last mustang. He talked to Senor Garcia and freed the bay mare, and then Senor Garcia walked back toward the house. Carlos would soon go to the big house for lunch. He would be hungry after working hard all morning. It was time for them to put their plan into action.

"Let us go," Angelica said beside her. "It is time."

Rosa nodded and together they started down the hill. Halfway down, they split up, Angelica to hurry around the outside of the ranch buildings and Rosa to march directly to the big house. She could feel her heart pounding faster and faster as she went. How was she going to form even simple words, let alone convince Senor Garcia? She'd never had the courage to speak more than four words to him before. In fact, usually when he was near she felt totally and completely tongue-tied.

But I have to do it. This is the plan we decided on, so I have to be tough, she commanded herself. *It's a good plan and if it works, everything will turn out perfectly.*

It *was* a good plan. Rosa would talk to Senor Garcia while Angelica sent the thought message that they hoped would soften his heart, and even if Senor Garcia didn't agree to give Lost Canyon to the mustangs, he might be influenced enough to free them and chase them from his land.

If Angelica's thought messages didn't touch him, didn't make him relent on either request, Rosa would flip her right braid over her shoulder, and Angelica would rush from her hiding place in the barn to throw the corral gate wide open. Senor Garcia still wouldn't think that Rosa had anything to do with freeing the mustangs, and her parents' jobs would be safe. Only the crazy blonde girl would be blamed, and she'd be gone with the wild ones. It was a foolproof plan – if she could just force herself to talk to Senor Garcia!

Too soon, Rosa reached the front door. Slowly, almost against her will, she raised her hand to grab the knocker. And stopped. She still didn't know what she

95

should say, how she would form the words. In fact, her mind felt numb, completely and totally blank. Desperately, she glanced back toward the barn. There was no sign of Angelica. She was probably in place, patiently waiting for Rosa to do her part. If only she could send Rosa some courage.

She's doing enough without having to help me. I'm not a baby, Rosa thought with self-contempt. *I need to get tougher. Remember Vivo. I can't let him die. Think of Rojo and Linda. Think of the foals. Do it for all of them!*

With a swift movement, Rosa grabbed the knocker and dropped it. And again. The sound echoed through the house. There was no going back now. She would have to think of something to say, and quick.

"Please don't let Mama answer the door. Please make her busy getting Carlos' lunch. Please," she prayed beneath her breath.

The doorknob turned and the massive wooden door swung open. Senor Garcia stood just inside, looking down on Rosa. She felt herself shrink beneath his gaze.

Now, she told herself. *Talk now.* But nothing came out of her mouth.

"Si?" Senor Garcia demanded.

"Uh." She swallowed and her face turned red. "Uh."

"What do you want?"

But Rosa couldn't say a word.

Rosa

"What do you want?" Senor Garcia repeated impatiently.

"Senor," croaked Rosa. Her breath came anxious and quick. "Sen… Senor," she tried again. She was suddenly aware of how incredibly hot she felt, of the sun blasting mercilessly down on the top of her head. More than anything, she wished she could melt into the doorstep and disappear.

Senor Garcia's glower increased and lines furrowed deeper into his weathered face. He crossed his arms over his chest.

Rosa shut her eyes. *Just pretend I'm talking to Papa,* she thought. *Just pretend.* "I need to talk to you about the mustangs," she said in a rush.

"What's that? Speak up."

She gathered her courage again. "I need to talk to you about the mustangs," she repeated a little louder.

"What about them?" The words were clipped and irate.

Rosa didn't dare open her eyes. Senor Garcia might think she was strange, but that was better than her not being able to speak. "They're living creatures, Senor. They don't deserve to die." She could have kicked herself. Why did she say it like that? She sounded as if

97

she was accusing him of being a murderer. But then, in a way, she was, wasn't she?

Senor Garcia didn't respond immediately and Rosa opened her eyes a crack. He was looking down at her as if it was the first time he'd seen her. "Liana thought the way you do. She never could understand that they're not like the ranch horses," he snapped and his gazed moved to look behind her. "They're not like your Ciervo. They're wild animals."

Rosa heard hoofbeats and turned. Ciervo! The gelding had grown tired of waiting for them at the pool. He nickered a greeting and stopped beside her. With Ciervo less than an arm's length away, Rosa felt braver. "They're living beings and they have lives to live too," she said to Senor Garcia. "And they're beautiful."

The man was quiet for a long moment. "Despite what you think, I'm not a monster," he finally said, his voice slightly less annoyed. Was Angelica's magic working on him? "I don't enjoy killing horses, even mustangs," he continued. "It's just the practical thing to do. You must see that."

Rosa shook her head, mutely.

"Come with me," he continued. "I want to show you something." He strode toward the corrals, leaving Rosa and Ciervo to follow. Rosa kept her left hand on Ciervo's neck as they trailed behind. Her right hand played with her braid as she walked, twisting it around and around her fingers. All she had to do was flip it over her shoulder and Angelica would free the horses. But she should wait. There was only a slim chance Senor Garcia would change his mind, but a slim chance was better than none. And besides, the ranch owner was too near the corrals now.

Rosa inhaled sharply when she saw the mustangs. They'd been divided into two herds! Four of the mares, including Linda and Vivo's palomino sister, were in a smaller corral while Rojo paced the fence in a larger pen. Vivo and the others stood behind him.

With a sinking feeling, Rosa realized the implications of two corrals – two gates to open. Now more than ever, their efforts to convince Senor Garcia had to work. If it didn't, Angelica may not have time to open two corral gates before she was stopped.

"You see those horses?" Senor Garcia said and pointed to the corral with the four mares. "I've already decided to keep them."

Rosa blinked in surprise. The ranch owner had relented, if just a bit. "But what about the others?" she asked, her voice shaking.

"Senor Domingo is coming to get them."

"Please, Senor." Rosa forced herself to speak again. Desperation lent strength to her voice. This was her last chance to convince him, she could feel it. "I'm asking you to set them free. They want to live. And you don't need to worry about them eating your grass. They'll stay at the back of that canyon. It's only such a little bit of grass and I've heard the cattle don't go there anyway. Or they can leave the ranch if you want. But Senor, they don't deserve to die." She could feel tears well up in her eyes and tried to blink them back. She didn't want to appear weak.

"They won't all die," Senor Garcia said in a clipped tone. "We're keeping the four."

"But why not all of them?"

"We don't need more. And the younger ones will take too long to grow up."

99

"But Vivo…" She clamped her mouth shut. The words had popped out before she could stop them.

"Who?"

"No one."

"Who?" All gentleness was gone from Senor Garcia's voice.

"The cremello," Rosa whispered, and looked down at the ground. "The two-year-old."

"You know these horses?" he asked, his voice as hard as flint.

"I… I've seen them before," Rosa confessed. "I've been watching them."

"And why didn't you say anything? Did you tell your parents?"

Rosa looked up. Desperation made her daring. "I didn't tell them anything," she said and directed her gaze firmly into Senor Garcia's eyes. "I didn't tell anyone. No one but me knew the mustangs were there." *And Angelica,* she thought. *But she doesn't count.*

"Why didn't you tell me?"

Rosa blinked back her tears again before she answered. "Because I knew this would happen. I knew you'd sell them to Senor Domingo, just like you wanted to… " Emotion choked off her voice for a moment, and she stared down at the ground with blurred vision. "Just like you wanted to sell Ciervo," she finally continued, then finished in a whisper. "I knew you'd want to kill them."

Senor Garcia

Senor Garcia frowned. He couldn't understand the girl's point of view but he'd heard it before. From Liana. In fact, it amazed him how similar their viewpoints were. And honestly, hadn't he enjoyed watching the mustangs the day before? Hadn't he been entertained by the antics of the two foals?

But that didn't matter. To think like that was weak. The mustangs ate too much, and he needed the grass for his cattle. And besides, he already had plans for the canyon meadow. It was the perfect place to fatten his yearling cattle before shipping them to market.

But he didn't want to be the monster in yet another girl's eyes. He looked down at Jose's daughter and scowled. She looked like she was about to cry! What would he say then? He'd always felt so helpless around crying girls. There had to be some way to make her happy, some way that wouldn't cost too much.

The fact that she liked that two-year-old was an opportunity. And if he gave her the colt, he wouldn't be doing anything wrong – obviously Jose didn't care that his daughter was gallivanting all over the countryside on the back of a horse. And if the girl's father didn't care, why should he? Besides, he liked the idea of being the hero, for a change.

Rosa

"You like horses?" Senor Garcia suddenly asked.

Rosa sniffled. What did that have to do with freeing the mustangs? "Si, Senor. I love horses," she said and wiped tears from her eyes.

"You seem to. I see you riding Ciervo all over. And you're a good rider. Would you like to learn more about horses?"

"Si, Senor," Rosa said. Was Senor Garcia going to relent? Was he going to free the mustangs?

"Okay, then." The man turned back toward the house. Carlos was leaning against the wall near the side door, relaxing in the shade as he ate a burrito. "Carlos!" Senor Garcia called and beckoned to him.

The horse wrangler popped the last bite of burrito into his mouth as he walked toward them. "Si, boss?"

"Put that light colored colt in with the four we're keeping. He's for Jose's girl. She's going to help you with the mustangs. They seem calm enough for her to handle, and she can do a lot of the gentling work. It'll free you up to do the harder stuff, and in return, she'll get the colt to keep."

Rosa could hardly breathe. Vivo would be hers to keep forever!

"Si, senor," said Carlos. He winked at Rosa. "It'll be good to have an assistant. She can get them used to all sorts of things. And there ain't no reason she can't do the halter breaking. She can groom them, too. I bet she'll have them looking like show horses in no time. You won't recognize them in another week."

Rosa smiled back at him. What a wonderful opportunity!

"Sounds good," Senor Garcia said beside her. Carlos nodded, tipped his hat, and turned back to the corrals. He opened the gate to the doomed mustangs' corral. "Well, go help him," the ranch owner said to Rosa.

Within a couple minutes, Rosa and Carlos had cut Vivo from Rojo's group and herded him into the mares' corral. The two-year-old crowded up next to his palomino sister and looked back at the two humans with wide eyes. He pricked his ears as they pushed the gate shut behind him.

Rosa turned to see Senor Garcia leaning on the corral fence, watching them with a half smile on his face. Taking a deep breath, she approached him. "Thank you, Senor," she said, and she really meant it. Except for Ciervo, she'd never been given such a wonderful gift. "Thank you so much."

The man nodded acknowledgement and turned back to the ranch house. He'd only gone a few steps, when Rosa gasped. How could she have forgotten about the others so easily? What was wrong with her? Without a thought of the consequences, she clambered through the rails and ran after him. "Senor!" she called out, her voice panicky.

Senor Garcia looked back.

Rosa came to a quick halt. "What about the other mustangs?"

"They go with Domingo," the man said, his voice flat and emotionless, then he stalked on to the house.

Rosa stood as if stunned. Senor Garcia had somehow turned the situation into one in which almost everyone was happy. He'd offered her the job of her dreams and given her a beautiful colt as payment. He'd let Carlos have his smart, tough saddle horses and an assistant. He'd let her mother and father keep their jobs even though he could never be sure they didn't know of the mustangs beforehand. And he'd given five of the twelve mustangs new lives. Almost everyone involved in the situation was a winner – except the seven mustangs he planned to sell to Senor Domingo. They would die. She had to give the signal to Angelica.

"You might as well start with your colt, Rosa," said Carlos from behind her. With her thoughts going a mile a minute, she turned to face him. "Just get him used to you, at first," Carlos continued. "Stand in the corral and talk to him. You can get one of the brushes from the barn to use in case he lets you close…"

Rosa stopped listening. She could see this would be their last chance to free the mustangs. Carlos was excited to have the horses to work with and would go back to the corral as soon as he finished talking to her. Though she and Carlos were standing only a few yards from the corrals, it was probably the farthest he'd be from the mustangs for hours. And soon Senor Domingo would arrive to load the discarded mustangs and Bonita into the back of his truck.

Rosa nodded to Carlos as if she was agreeing with whatever he was saying, and flipped her right braid over her shoulder.

Rosa

Angelica emerged from the barn behind Carlos like a golden blur. Rosa looked back at the horse wrangler's face the moment she saw the older girl, her gaze as innocent as she could make it, but something in her expression must have betrayed her. Carlos spun around.

"Who's that?" he asked, surprised. "What's she doing?"

Angelica raced to the gate of the closest corral, the one holding the mustangs to be sold to Senor Domingo. She struggled with the catch on the gate for a moment, just long enough for Carlos to realize what she was doing. "Hey!" he yelled and ran toward her.

Rosa was amazed at how quickly he covered the ground as he raced toward the corral. She clasped her hands together over her heart.

Angelica jerked back on the heavy wood, finally having released the latch, and the gate began to swing open. With a swirl of golden hair, she raced on to the second corral.

Rojo herded his small group toward freedom as the gate glided open, and the mares pushed their foals before them. A chestnut foal ran through the gate, followed by a black yearling – and then Carlos was between the horses and freedom, waving his arms and yelling. The rest of the herd spun back and Carlos pushed the gate shut behind them.

With the second group, Angelica was successful. All five horses streamed between the gateposts. The girl leapt astride the last mare to burst from the corral, a stout bay and white pinto. Her hair flashed chocolate and white, and then she and the mustangs disappeared in a cloud of dust. Carlos ran behind them, yelling, though there was obviously nothing he could do to stop them.

Moments later, the air was filled with the searing cries of the herd left behind. The five captive mustangs galloped around and around their corral, heads and tails high in distress.

"What's going on here?"

Rosa gasped and spun around to see Senor Garcia striding toward her with a glowering face. When his gaze lifted to the dusty corral, his expression became even more severe. "What happened?" he barked.

"A... a girl, a stranger, ran out of the barn and opened the gates. Carlos stopped most of the horses from escaping," Rosa said, trying to keep the disappointment from her voice. If only the hired hand hadn't been so quick. "But the mustangs you wanted to keep got away."

"Is that right?" Senor Garcia said, looking past Rosa.

She almost said 'si' but then Carlos mumbled behind her. "Sorry, Senor." Rosa turned to see the horse wrangler approaching with hat in hand, his gaze locked on the ground and shoulders stooped. Behind him, the corralled mustangs slowed to a trot.

106

Senor Garcia shook his head and made an exasperated sound. "It wasn't your fault, Carlos," he finally said.

"We could train the one's we still have," suggested the ranch hand hopefully.

"No," said Senor Garcia, in a brisk, businesslike tone. "Senor Domingo will be here soon and they can go with him. We'll catch the others and bring them back. It shouldn't be hard. They'll probably head straight back to Lost Canyon. It's their home ground."

"Si, Senor."

"And keep a guard on the corrals until Domingo gets here," the ranch owner added. "Just in case this girl comes back."

"I'll stay with them, Senor."

A tiny whinny floated toward them and Rosa spun around to see the chestnut pinto mare charge toward her prison fence. Her relieved neigh drowned all other sounds as the chestnut foal trotted out of the dust left by the escaping mustangs. He'd come back to his dam!

Please, baby, turn back, Rosa prayed. She ached to run toward him, waving her arms and yelling, but she knew it wouldn't do any good. If Angelica hadn't convinced the baby to stay with the freed mustangs – and she was sure the enchantress would've tried – then how could she? The mare nickered to her baby and leaned over the fence to nuzzle his neck. Tears pooled in Rosa's eyes as she watched. They were so happy to see one another. And totally unaware of the horror they would soon be facing together.

I have to try one more time. I just can't let the beautiful baby and his mother die. Or any of the others. Surely, the sight of the two being reunited had touched

Senor Garcia as well. "Senor Garcia, will you *please* change your mind?" she asked tearfully.

There was no answer. She turned around. The ranch owner was halfway back to the house, striding away from her and Carlos with a strong step.

Behind her, the stallion sent one more loud call after his escaped family. A final farewell? In the silence that followed, Carlos sighed.

Senor Garcia

Senor Garcia smiled as he strode back to his house. Clearly, Carlos wasn't the one who'd tried to free the mustangs last night. It was this blonde girl, probably an American girl, one of those crazy people who believe they can save the world. And the horses hadn't been drugged either. If they had, they wouldn't have reacted so quickly to the opened gate.

He was so relieved that Carlos hadn't betrayed him that he hardly cared the mustangs had been freed. They'd be easy to catch again anyway, as long as they stayed on the ranch. And if they didn't? Well then, they weren't his problem. Some other rancher would have to deal with them.

Yet, as he opened the front door to his house and stepped inside, he felt a strange sense of loss. He shivered in the coolness of the foyer. No mustangs on his ranch – it was a good thing. So why did he feel like he was missing something?

It was that girl's fault; she was confusing him. She was so much like Liana. Not in her appearance, but in her ideas. She wanted to give Lost Canyon to the mustangs. What a ridiculous suggestion!

"Why can't they understand that it goes against common sense?" he whispered.

"Pardon, Senor?" A woman's voice. The girl's mother. "What did you say?" She was polishing the table in the corner of the spacious entranceway, and he'd been so preoccupied that he hadn't seen her.

"I said nothing, Senora Fernandez," he answered, his face hot with embarrassment. He re-adopted his commanding stride and moved toward his office.

Enough silliness. Enough. Enough. Enough. He'd wasted enough thought, energy, and dignity on these vermin mustangs. The sooner they were gone, the better.

Rosa

Without a word, Carlos turned back to the corral. Rosa barely noticed his dejected bearing. Her mind was on other things, like how she was to save the rest of the mustangs. Angelica would be busy with those she'd freed from the corrals for a while, and though Carlos might want the mustangs to be saved, there was no point in talking to him about it. He obviously wasn't about to go against Senor Garcia's directives. In fact, Rosa couldn't help but feel a bit of resentment toward the hired hand. If he wanted to help the mustangs so much, why hadn't he run just a bit slower when Angelica was freeing them?

She scuffed the ground with a dusty shoe. She didn't have time to blame Carlos. She had to think of some way to save the horses, and do it without Angelica helping her for a while, without Carlos stopping her, without Senor Garcia knowing she was involved, and without failing this time. And quickly, too. It was already after one o'clock. Senor Domingo would be there within the hour.

Ciervo nuzzled her shoulder and she turned to lean her forehead against his. "Hey, amigo," she whispered. "Do you have any ideas?" The gelding snorted, lowered his head further and looked up at her with hopeful eyes. Rosa sighed. "Me neither. Let's go for a quick ride. It'll help me think."

She looked back once as they rode from the ranch yard. Carlos was leaning on the corral fence, watching the mustangs. Even from a distance, he looked depressed. The horses crowded against the far side of the corral, their heads raised in anxiety as they watched him watching them.

Rosa's attention jerked forward as Ciervo sprung into a canter. Swiftly he carried her away from the ranch buildings, his stride lengthening and shortening as he wove through the cacti. The air whipped around them as they picked up speed and Rosa's eyes watered in the hot wind.

What was she going to do? She had to figure it out!

What about after Senor Domingo loads the horses into his truck? She tightened the reins and Ciervo shortened his stride. *Maybe there's something I can do to free them after they're away from the ranch house? That way Senor Garcia won't know I'm involved and Carlos can't stop us.*

In her mind's eye, she pictured the driveway to the ranch buildings, just the way it appeared from the bluff at Rattlesnake Rock. From her favorite perch, the narrow road looked like a long snake winding from the ranch to the distant highway. Was there something she could do to stop Senor Domingo along the driveway?

Maybe she and Angelica could use a variation of their last plan. She could distract the driver while the enchantress freed the mustangs at the back of his truck. Rosa was sure Senor Domingo wouldn't recognize her. During his few visits to the ranch, he'd never paid much attention to her except when she was riding

Ciervo, and then his eyes had been watching the gelding, not her. If she was careful to keep out of sight whenever he came back to the ranch, he would probably never associate the freeing of the mustangs to her – and that meant her parents' jobs would be safe.

Rosa reined the gelding in the direction of Rattlesnake Rock. It wasn't a foolproof plan, not like the last one had appeared to be. Far too many things could go wrong. But it was the best she could think of, and almost any idea, no matter how poor, was better than no idea at all.

Ciervo breathed heavily as he clambered up the incline toward the bluff edge. Rosa clung to him like a burr as he lurched up the slope. When they finally topped the hill, the horse slowed to catch his breath and Rosa cast an anxious eye along the driveway winding past below them. Thank goodness, there was no sign of Senor Domingo's truck. Yet.

"We have to hurry, amigo," she murmured and patted Ciervo's sweaty shoulder. The gelding puffed in time to his hoofbeats as he cantered along the abrupt edge. Quickly, they drew near their destination: the coal black rock balanced at the edge of the bluff. As they approached, the white streak on its surface seemed to rise up higher, exactly like a rattlesnake preparing to strike.

Rosa pulled Ciervo to a quick stop when she spied the distant puff of dust. It could only be one thing: Senor Domingo's truck. He was early!

For a second, she couldn't breathe. The immensity of the task before them was overwhelming. How was she going to stop the truck and distract the driver long enough for Angelica to free the mustangs? Should she simply stand in the middle of the road and wave her arms? Or maybe she could pretend she was injured.

But then what do I do after Angelica gallops away with the horses? The question sent an arrow of fear through her heart. Unless she could escape afterward as well, Senor Domingo would take her back to the ranch – and everyone would know she had helped free the mustangs. Rosa squeezed her eyes shut. It was hopeless. There was no way to both free the horses and escape herself.

But maybe Angelica will have a better idea. Instantly, Rosa felt better. Of course, Angelica would know what to do. She breathed deeply and touched the necklace – and it barely tingled against her fingers! With dread, she remembered the drain of energy she'd experienced the last time she'd used it. Did the necklace even have enough power left to summon Angelica? And if not, would it suck the energy it needed from Rosa? Would she be left even weaker than last time, unable to do anything to help the mustangs? Or herself?

Why, oh why, couldn't something go right for a change?

Stop! Please stop! Let me slip from your back, my love. Rosa is about to call me. I can feel her need reaching out to me as she touches her weakened necklace. If I do not hurry, she will attempt to summon me, despite the cost to her own being. I must use my own energy to go to her. And I must remember to give her another necklace before I leave her this time.

My dears, you must carry on in this direction until you reach the ocean, and then follow the beaches north. Keep watch for the rest of your herd. If all goes well, we will join you soon.

And, my loves, I know it is hard to hear, but if Rosa and I are unsuccessful, the rest of your family will never come. If this happens, you must carry on, look forward only. You must gallop many, many miles from here. Though humans are everywhere, you must search for a hidden place, a new and safe home.

I wish you luck. I wish you peace. And until we meet again, farewell, my loves.

Rosa

This time Rosa kept her eyes open to watch for the enchantress's appearance. "I need you, Angelica," she whispered. "Can you hear me? Where are you? Can you come?" The tingle between her fingers spiked and Rosa felt the same painful tug at her heart as before, the same draining of her energy.

No! The refusal was automatic. She didn't want to give away her energy, her life force. The tingling faded. And so did the self-contained glowing that hung in the air before her.

I have to try again! Tentatively, she opened herself to the pull. A quiet hum vibrated around her, then was drowned out by the rumble of Senor Domingo's truck passing below the bluff.

A flash of golden light burst before her! Rosa would have fallen backward if she'd been standing. When she lowered her protective hand, Angelica was standing there, fully embodied, and smiling at her.

"How... But..." No more words would come from Rosa's mouth.

"Do not be frightened," said Angelica, seeing the shock on the younger girl's face. "I am the same as I was last time you saw me. I have not changed."

Of course, she hasn't. Get a grip, Rosa commanded herself. *Angelica isn't the enemy.* She slipped from

116

Ciervo's back and cleared her throat. "How are the mustangs?" she said in as normal a voice as she could muster.

"They are on their way to safety," Angelica answered. "What happened after we escaped?"

"Senor Garcia is sending Rojo's group with Senor Domingo. And he's here now." She pointed to the dust trail moving toward the distant ranch buildings. "That was his truck that just passed. He's early. We need to think of a plan quick. I had one, but I don't know if it will work now."

"What is your idea?"

Quickly, Rosa explained.

Angelica's brow creased in concentration and she twirled a strand of hair around her index finger. Once, twice, three times. "I think I know another way."

Senor Garcia

Senor Domingo's brakes screeched as his huge truck stopped in front of the ranch house. Senor Garcia ground his teeth as he walked to the front door.

"Buenos dias, Senor!" Senor Domingo greeted the ranch owner when he walked from the house.

"Buenos dias, Senor Domingo. How are you?" the ranch owner responded, his words clipped.

The pudgy man straightened his sombrero before responding. "I am well, Senor Garcia. And how are you on this fine day?"

"I am well." Senor Garcia motioned toward the corral. "There are only six..." His gaze caught that of the red stallion, and the challenge in the dark eyes leapt across the distance between them. Quickly, he turned away. "There are only six for you today, Senor," he said brusquely. "No, seven," he added, remembering the old mare in the barn.

The slaughterer rubbed his hands together. "You said there were thirteen, Senor, and of that bunch, I only see four good-sized mustangs."

"I'll throw in the two foals for nothing," said Senor Garcia, not wanting to haggle. The sooner the horses were gone, the better. He could almost feel the stallion's eyes drilling into the back of his head. "Just

give me the same price per horse that you paid last time, and I'll not say another word."

Senor Domingo opened his mouth as if to argue, then closed it with a snap. The offer of two free foals was apparently too good to pass up. He reached into his pocket, pulled out his wallet, and laid five worn bills in Senor Garcia's hand.

"I must return to my work now, Senor, but Carlos will help you." The ranch owner didn't wait for the slaughterer's response. Suddenly, he was feeling ill. His chest tightened as he hurried away and slipped inside his house.

He leaned back against the closed front door, relieved that it was almost over. The mustangs would be gone in just a few minutes.

Yet even with the door between them, he could hear the thud of their hooves. They were running around their corral, trying in vain to escape the truck backing toward them. He could hear their frightened neighs – and they sounded reproachful, condemning, accusing.

But that's impossible. They're just horses.

And besides, I've done nothing wrong!

Rosa

Angelica's new idea improved Rosa's plan, and for the first time since she'd ridden from the ranch, the younger girl felt there was a chance they'd succeed. *If* everything worked perfectly, they would free the mustangs without jeopardizing anyone or anything. The beauty of Angelica's plan was that neither girl would cause the diversion. Instead, they would block the driveway leading from the ranch and when the truck full of horses stopped at the obstacle, they'd sneak to the back of the truck, free the mustangs, and ride away, Rosa on Bonita and Angelica on one of the wild horses.

It was Ciervo who'd shown them what the diversion could be. As the girls stood watching the dust billow up behind Senor Domingo's truck, wracking their brains on the best way to create an obstacle, a sharp sound came from behind them. They spun around to see Ciervo's front hoof flash out a second time and strike the base of the balancing rock.

"That is it," exclaimed Angelica. "That is our diversion."

Rosa knew what she meant right away. "Si," she whispered. "Let's get to work."

Senor Garcia

The office walls seemed to press against Senor Garcia as he tried to concentrate on his paperwork. He leaned over to shut a file drawer and heard the snort of a horse in the movement. He picked up some papers from his desk and heard the sound of Liana's voice. He closed his eyes for a moment and saw the red stallion staring at him.

He jumped up and started to pace back and forth. Was that the thunder of hooves he could hear? He stopped short in the middle of the room and listened. He was sure he could hear them – running, snorting, neighing, as they tried to escape the slaughterer. And suddenly he realized the sound was the thud of his own heart. The whistle of his own breath.

Am I going crazy? What have these horses done to me?

The sound that answered his thought wasn't imagined. Senor Domingo's unmuffled engine revved as the truck roared away from the ranch buildings, the mustangs undoubtedly inside. The slaughterer had finished loading the horses.

Senor Garcia stood still, breathlessly waiting, for the sound to die in the distance. Finally, they were gone. It was finished, at last. He breathed a sigh of relief.

121

And then he heard it – and somehow he knew he was the only one who could – a foal's whinny. And another. An image of the two foals he'd just sent to death catapulted into his mind: the colt, a red chestnut with three white socks, the filly, a black with a white snip coming out of her left nostril. How could he remember them in such detail? But worse than these was what he imagined next – the sorrel mare, Bonita, looking at him with dark, sad eyes, reminding him with a glance of the times she'd carried him on her back.

I have to get out of here!

Senor Garcia almost ran from his office. He hurried across the tiled foyer toward the front door. He'd take Macho out for a ride. That would make him feel better. The wind created by a good gallop would chase these strange cobwebs from his brain. He'd done the right thing with the mustangs. He must have. They were worthless horses. They had no value.

"As a man in a position of power, I have to make hard decisions, Liana," he whispered. "And I have to stick with them."

He clamped trembling lips together when he realized he'd spoken aloud, to someone who wasn't even there. But that didn't change the truth of what he'd said. He had made a hard decision and he did have to stick with it.

And now he would live with his choice.

Rosa

Rosa threw her weight against the balanced stone. It didn't even shudder. She timed her next heave to coincide with Angelica's, and again Rattlesnake Rock stood firm. But they couldn't quit. They had to push the rock off the bluff if their plan was going to work!

Rosa spoke between gritted teeth as she shoved against the unyielding stone, "Maybe if we move… some of the small rocks… from the other side… it'll go over." Sweat ran into her eyes, making them burn, and her muscles felt like jelly. She collapsed against the unmoving rock, her arms quivering with fatigue. Wearily, she raised her hand to wipe the sweat away. Angelica leaned beside her and closed her eyes. For the first time since Rosa had met the girl, she was breathing faster than normal.

Rosa looked back toward the ranch. There was no sign of the truck. They still had time, but not much. It wouldn't take Senor Domingo long to chase the horses through the corral gate and into the back of the truck, or to load poor Bonita.

"Moving some of the smaller stones is a good idea," Angelica agreed and pushed herself upright. "I will do it." She disappeared around the side of the rock.

Rosa followed her. "Careful," she said when Angelica knelt at the edge of the bluff and leaned out to loosen the stones.

One small rock bounced noisily down the slope and another larger stone tumbled behind it. The two rocks struck more stones as they plunged downward and soon a cavalcade of stones was tumbling down the hill. Angelica pulled back from the edge and the two girls watched the avalanche until it slid to a halt below.

"Let's try again," suggested Rosa, a renewed enthusiasm in her voice.

But despite their best efforts, the gigantic stone remained firm. As the minutes ticked by, Rosa's movements became more desperate and less effective. She kept glancing along the driveway toward the ranch expecting at any moment to see the dust from Senor Domingo's truck driving toward them.

And then she saw it. The cloud of dust was miniscule in the distance, yet the sight of it struck at her heart. The horse slaughterer was coming. They were almost out of time. Beside her, Angelica straightened. Together they watched the tiny puff of dust grow larger.

"What are we going to do?" whispered Rosa. "We're not strong enough to push the rock off the edge and there's no other way to block the driveway."

"I do not know," said Angelica. Silence. Ciervo snorted.

Rosa strained to hear the sound of the truck, but it was still too far away. They might still have time to do something, if they could think of another way to block the road. But really, Rosa knew, there was only one other way. "I have to stop him by pretending to be injured," she said with a sinking heart. Ciervo snorted again.

"No. Let me stop him. You can free the horses at the back," protested Angelica. "There is more evil that can happen if you are caught. If your parents are fired from their jobs and you have to leave the ranch, they may be forced to sell Ciervo. And that would break his heart. I must be the one to create the diversion."

Rosa almost cried. In all her worries about leaving the ranch, she hadn't considered this one thing. But it was true; if her parents didn't have a paycheck, they couldn't afford to keep Ciervo. They'd be forced to sell him. She could almost imagine Senor Domingo's glee when the gelding went up for sale. Angelica was right. Rosa had to be the one to free the mustangs.

But could she do it alone? Was she strong enough to open the back of the truck without help? And then she had to catch Bonita without a rope and mount her without a mounting block, because the tall mare wasn't trained to lower her neck and slide Rosa onto her back. And to do it all without Senor Domingo catching her? Or even seeing her?

She noticed movement out of the corner of her eye. Ciervo was backing toward her. "What are you doing, amigo?" Surprised, she stepped back. The warmth of Rattlesnake Rock pressed against her shoulder blades. The horse backed another step and turned his head to look at her with white-rimmed eyes. "What's wrong with him, Angelica?" Rosa asked, mystified.

"But why did I not think to ask him? He is by far the strongest among us." Angelica sounded as if she were scolding herself. "Come this way, Rosa." She grabbed the younger girl's hand and pulled her away from the rock. Together they watched Ciervo back until his hindquarters touched the rock. "See? He is helping us push," explained Angelica, when the big gelding leaned against the rock.

The girls didn't waste any time. They sprung to either side of Ciervo and pushed with all the strength they could muster. For a moment, the rock didn't move – and then it shifted beneath Rosa's hands. She felt like cheering when the massive stone slowly tipped toward the edge of the bluff.

The rock fell like a giant tree. Slowly at first, then faster and faster. It picked up speed as it thundered down the incline, loosening rocks, dirt, and other debris to crash along in its wake. Less than halfway down the slope, the tumbling mass was lost in a billowing cloud of dust.

Senor Domingo would see the dust from the landslide, Rosa knew. She looked in the direction of the truck. The slaughterer was getting close. There was no time to celebrate their accomplishment. They needed to get into position. The next phase of their plan was the most crucial of all.

Senor Garcia

Macho shied mid stride, almost throwing Senor Garcia from his back. The man recovered quickly and reined the big gelding to a halt, then looked back. What had caused Macho to jump like that? It wasn't like him to be skittish, and the man could see nothing amiss.

The gelding snorted and pawed the ground, then looked to the right with his ears pricked forward. Senor Garcia followed his gaze. A distant billowing cloud of dust, a faint rumble. A slide on the bluffs? It looked near Rattlesnake Rock. Had the rock fallen?

Senor Garcia frowned. Just what he needed – another problem. Maybe the slide was harmless, but then maybe it had covered the driveway too. Years ago, a much smaller stone had rolled down the bluff, creating a landslide. All vehicle traffic to and from the ranch had stopped for a week.

As Senor Garcia reined Macho toward the bluffs, he remembered Senor Domingo. Surely, the slaughterer had already driven past the slide area. He certainly hoped so – but it would be just his luck lately to have both the unlikeable man and the mustangs stuck at the ranch until the driveway was cleared.

But he was jumping to conclusions. The road might not be blocked at all. That was the first thing to check.

127

Rosa

Rosa stroked Ciervo on his neck and gave him a quick hug. "Thank you so much, Ciervo. We couldn't have done it without you," she whispered into the gelding's ear. "But you have to go home now. If Senor Domingo sees you watching from up here, he'll recognize you."

She tightened her arms around Ciervo's strong neck one more time before releasing him, then patted him on his hindquarters. Reluctantly, the gelding moved off.

Angelica was waiting for her at the bluff edge. Rosa swung her legs over the edge and turned onto her stomach. They had to hurry. Senor Domingo was only a couple of miles away. Angelica grasped Rosa's arms for safety as the younger girl lowered herself down the drop-off at the top of the bluff. Her feet scrambled for a foothold, but at first all she could feel were loose stones and gravel that instantly gave way beneath her feet. Finally, her left foot found an outcropping that seemed stable. Tentatively she trusted her weight to it. It held.

"Just a little lower and you will be past the overhang," said Angelica, looking down over Rosa's shoulder. Her grip moved to Rosa's hands and she dropped even farther over the edge.

"Right here is good," she said when her feet touched the firmer rock and gravel at the top of the slope.

Slowly Angelica released her, and though the rocks shifted slightly beneath Rosa's feet, they didn't slide. A few moments later, Angelica was over the bluff and standing beside her.

"I think we should sit to slide down," suggested the golden girl, looking down the incline. "And we must go slowly. We do not want to create another rockslide."

Rosa nodded in agreement and lowered herself to the ground. The dust from the avalanche was so thick, she could scarcely see the road below, but she could make out the white "snake" quartz vein through the dust cloud. From its position, she guessed that Rattlesnake Rock had tumbled to a stop in the middle of the driveway. Perfect!

Together they scooted down the slide track on their bottoms. More dust rose around them, making Rosa sneeze as they descended. Pebbles clattered down the hill in front of them to join the debris at the bottom. Close to the bottom of the slide, the slope wasn't as steep and she stood to climb down the last few yards.

Finally safe at the bottom, she looked up at the slide and bluff behind them. Through the dust, she could see Ciervo peering over the edge at them.

"Go home now, Ciervo," she yelled. "We're fine." She coughed when dust caught in her throat. With a snort, the bay gelding pulled away from the bluff edge and disappeared. Rosa glanced at Angelica. "Senor Domingo will be here any second," she said. "Do you really think we can do this?"

Angelica smiled reassuringly but her words didn't sound as confident when she replied, "I hope so."

Senor Garcia

Senor Garcia noticed the horse the second he topped the rise. It was far away, too far to identify accurately, yet still, something about it was familiar. Something in the way it held its head, in the way it moved.

Ciervo! Could it be? If so, he was without a rider. What had happened to the girl? Had there been an accident? Was she lying injured somewhere?

He leaned forward, pushing Macho into a gallop. If he could catch the bay gelding, maybe there would be some clue as to where the girl might be.

His next thought left him breathless and he jerked the black to a sliding stop. What if the girl had been caught in the slide? Ciervo was trotting directly away from the dust still hanging in the air. What if the girl had been near the top of the bluff and the ground had broken away beneath her, tossing her down to tumble among the rocks and debris to the bottom? What if she'd been buried in the avalanche?

He yanked Macho back toward the slide and dug his spurs into the horse's side. He had to find her quick! The gelding leapt forward with a surprised snort, then leveled out into a dead run toward the bluff, Senor Garcia clinging to his back.

Rosa

Rosa crouched behind the largest stone at the side of the road. Angelica hunkered down beside her.

"He's going to see us," Rosa whispered to the older girl. In her opinion, she and Angelica were far too visible around the pale stone's edges. All Senor Domingo had to do was look away from the giant rock sprawled across the road, glance out the side window, and he would see them.

"He will not see us," Angelica whispered back.

"But Angelica, we're too big to hide behind this rock," she tried again.

"There is no other place to hide."

"Maybe we can dig down a bit, so there's a hole behind the rock, and hide that way." Rosa started to scoop the loose earth away from the back of the stone.

She stopped when Angelica touched her arm. "Trust me," her soft voice said. "He will not see us. I will… " A gasp cut her sentence short and she shrunk behind the too-small rock. Rosa crouched beside her. The rumble of an engine filled the air. "He is here," Angelica finished.

Senor Garcia

Senor Garcia stopped Macho near the edge of the bluff and looked across the expanse. The black horse pranced beneath him, eager to continue his run across the desert.

"Hold steady, boy," the man said and patted the gelding on the neck to calm him. With a snort of protest the horse stilled, and in the silence the man heard a vehicle approach from below the bluffs.

Swiftly, the ranch owner dismounted and, keeping one of Macho's long split reins in his grip, crept nearer the edge. As he'd guessed, the balancing rock had fallen, taking part of the hillside with it. He'd always wondered when it would happen. Though the rock must've stood there for centuries, he'd halfway expected it to fall for years. A huge stone, balanced on a small point, at the edge of a bluff – it made an impressive picture – but logic dictated that it wouldn't be overly stable. The only surprise was that it had stood there as long as it had.

He moved forward carefully. The rock's fall may have made the bluff edge unstable, and he certainly didn't want to feel the ground slide away beneath his own feet. Yet if he was to see over the edge, if he was to see if the girl was lying injured below, he had to get closer.

He could see Rattlesnake Rock below now, and then the slaughterer's truck too from his bird's-eye-view, slowly rolling closer to the giant rock. But he still didn't see the girl. Maybe she'd escaped the slide. Or had been buried in it.

She might still be closer to the bottom of the bluff, he realized. He had to take the chance and go right to the edge to peer over. But what if he saw her broken body among the stones? He couldn't imagine anything worse. And he would be responsible. If the daughter of his employees met an early death, simply because he hadn't recognized a dangerous situation on his own land, it would be his fault.

A sudden chill touched his spine in the stifling hot afternoon and he leaned forward. Si, he was seeing right. The clouds of dust from the slide were moving swiftly away. And yet he hadn't felt the slightest breeze up on the bluff. How was that possible?

Senor Domingo's truck brakes squealed again as he stopped short. The air was so clear that Senor Garcia could see every line on the slaughterer's face, despite the distance between them. But Senor Domingo's expression wasn't what the ranch owner would've expected. There was no irritation at finding the road blocked. No anger. Only round-eyed shock.

With sudden unease, Senor Garcia followed the man's gaze toward the rock. Macho's rein almost slid from his fingers.

The wind isn't blowing the dust away. It's moving it to a single point! Condensing it, right in front of the rock!

He watched, speechless, as the dust continued to gather. Rapidly, it became thicker and thicker, more and more solid, a dense writhing mass. He couldn't help but think of a living creature as he watched it, a creature with a true presence, a mind, and an energy all its own.

Then, as if the white snake on Rattlesnake Rock had come horribly alive, a thick chunk of solid dust broke from the mass to rise sinuously into the sky!

Rosa

Rosa kept as still as she could behind the rock. She just *knew* Senor Domingo was going to see them. Her only hope was that the descent down the slide had made her t-shirt dirty enough that the red wouldn't be so bright. But there was nothing that would hide the glisten of Angelica's hair. It would be like a beacon, pulling Senor Domingo's eyes to them. Then they would be caught, and the mustangs and Bonita would die.

She heard the squeal of Senor Domingo's brakes and knew it was over. He'd seen them. Any second she'd hear his yell, asking them what on earth they were doing, huddled behind that rock. What would she tell him? There was no logical response. At least none she could think of. She squeezed her eyes shut as she waited. But the yell didn't come.

Carefully, she raised her head to look over the too-small rock. Senor Domingo was sitting in his cab on the road in front of them, staring at the road ahead with his mouth hanging open and eyes wide in terror. He seemed frozen in fear. And Rosa could see why! A massive horse stood on top of Rattlesnake Rock. And this wasn't just any horse, one made of flesh and blood. It was made of dust!

"Do not be frightened," Angelica whispered beside her as the horse swung its humungous head from side to side, peering all the while into the cab of the slaughterer's truck with its glowing eyes. "Let us go."

Rosa hardly heard her. The dust horse was pawing the rock now. Only when the older girl's elbow bumped her arm was she able to tear her eyes away from strange beast. "You made that?" she whispered.

Angelica nodded. "Hurry," she said. "I cannot keep it going for long. It takes much of my energy."

Rosa and Angelica crept swiftly and soundlessly toward the truck and within seconds, were at the back, safely out of Senor Domingo's sight. No yells followed them. There was no sign they'd been spotted. Angelica was right. Senor Domingo hadn't seen them. And no wonder. The poor man was terrified. The two girls could have been standing in plain sight, waving bright flags and yelling, and he wouldn't have noticed them.

Rosa shook her head. She needed to get the vision of the dust horse out of her own mind too. It was time to think clearly, act quickly, and free the horses.

"Can you climb up?" asked Angelica, sounding weak and preoccupied. The dust horse must be swiftly draining her energy.

Rosa nodded and jumped up on the back bumper. She could see there was only one latch. When she lifted it, the door should swing open. With all the strength remaining to her, she jerked upward on the metal handle.

Senor Garcia

Senor Garcia backed a few steps from the bluff edge in astonishment. What was happening? This horse, this huge horse made of dust, was impossible. The wind couldn't play such tricks.

But my mind can. Is my mind playing tricks on me again? He didn't think so. Not unless Senor Domingo was having the same problem, the same vision. Obviously, he could see the dust horse as well.

So it had to be the wind. But he could hear no wind. He could feel no wind. The only sound was his own quick breathing, the only coolness was the terror shivering beneath his own skin and stealing into his mind, robbing him of logical thought. And how could the wind create glowing eyes?

Rosa

The latch didn't budge. Rosa felt like screaming with frustration. She hated being so weak! First the rock and now the latch.

"Wait." Angelica put her pale hands against the heavy door and pushed, relieving some of the pressure on the latch. "Try again," she whispered, her eyes closed.

"Are you okay?" Rosa asked. Angelica nodded and Rosa jerked upward again. This time the latch scraped halfway up – and the shriek of metal against metal sliced the air.

"He'll hear us!" Her voice was an urgent whisper.

Angelica was still leaning on the door, her eyes closed. "Again," she whispered, sounding half asleep. "We must hurry. The dust horse is falling."

Senor Garcia

There was a sudden unexplained sound of metal scraping against metal. Grateful to put his mind to practical use, Senor Garcia's eyes leaped to the man sitting mesmerized in his truck. Senor Domingo simply stared at the dust horse as it pawed the rock with a vaporous hoof. The slaughterer was as still as a stone, looking completely incapable of hearing the noise, let alone making it. So where had the sound come from?

It was then he noticed the two figures at the back of the truck. A smaller person had climbed up on the fender, but his attention was captured by the strange girl pushing on the back of the truck. Her golden hair shimmered in the heat as she shoved against the door. He knew her immediately. The mustang thief!

As suddenly as it had come, the fear cleared from his mind. This strange girl must have created the illusion to distract them – though he didn't understand how. But still, there was no doubt this must be her doing.

"Senor!" he yelled. The slaughterer stared straight ahead as the dust-horse began to dissipate into cloud, floating away and settling to the ground, bit by bit.

"Senor Domingo!" he tried again, louder. The man's startled face turned up to Senor Garcia. "Behind your truck! Hurry! They're stealing your mustangs!"

Rosa looked around in confusion. Someone was shouting, calling to Senor Domingo and warning him of their presence, but no one else was there.

"He is coming!" Angelica's whisper was harsh with urgency.

"Who? From where?" Rosa couldn't keep the panic from her voice.

"The driver!"

And Rosa heard the truck door slam shut. Alarm lent her strength as she jerked up on the door handle with all her might. The metal shrieked again and the latch popped open.

Rosa didn't have time to jump down before the door swung outward. The mustangs must have been pressing against the door! Instantly, she was pushed backward, arms and legs flailing.

The breath burst from her lungs upon impact and instantly Rosa felt an unbelievable pain shoot through her body. She curled into a ball, her eyes wide and mouth open, gasping uselessly for air she couldn't inhale. Angelica tugged on her arm, but she couldn't rise. The older girl's mouth moved but Rosa only heard the rush of her own blood roaring in her ears. All she could think was of wanting air more than anything she'd ever wanted in her life – but she couldn't breathe. Her lungs refused to inhale. She was going to die!

In a fog, she watched a mustang sail over her head, perfectly silhouetted against an azure sky. And another. Another. Angelica released her arm and spun away from her. And then the sky was swallowed by an expanding grayness, the mustangs became mere ghosts, and even the bright girl was hidden in shadows.

Rosa

Noises first ventured inside the greyness, the sound of hooves thundering around her. Then she felt hands pushing her to a sitting position. And she was breathing! She hadn't died. The breath had just been knocked out of her. She inhaled with half-aware relief as an electric grip lifted her to a broad back. Long, tangled mane was pushed between her limp fingers and she was conscious of a brightness on the other side of her eyelids.

"Go now! Run! All of you!"

Rosa's eyes popped open, and instantly clamped shut. What was that bright light? That incredible glowing? Then, just as suddenly, the light was gone. The horse she was riding moved forward, slowly and carefully, as if purposefully trying not to upset her. She opened her eyes to find herself lying forward across the red shoulders and black mane of the small bay mare, the dam of the black filly. A mustang! What had happened to Bonita?

She sat upright and tightened her fingers around the long hair just in time. The mare leapt into a gallop. In front of them, another bay mare, the chestnut pinto and her colt, and Bonita powered forward over the desert.

Rosa heard a yell from behind and looked back. The black filly was right behind her mount, stuck to the

142

mare's haunches like glue. And at the back of the truck, she could see Senor Domingo, with Angelica in his grip! He held the limp girl in front of him in an effort to ward off the angry stallion. As Rosa watched, Rojo reared up and struck out at the man, and narrowly missed Angelica's head.

"Let her go!" Rosa yelled but there was no response. The man didn't even look up. Had he heard her? She had to turn around. She had to help Angelica. The girl looked as if she barely had enough strength to stand.

Suddenly Senor Domingo let Angelica go. She slumped to the ground as he spun around and ran around the side of his truck. Rojo snorted and reared again, then trotted to stand over the girl. He lowered his head to sniff at her and then Rosa was carried over the crest of a small hill and the scene behind her disappeared.

We have to save her! We have to go back!

"Come on, horse," she crooned to the wild mare and tugged on her mane. "Turn back. Turn back." The mare pinned her ears and snorted, but she didn't slow down.

Rosa looked back again and a movement on the bluff caught her attention. Her heart lurched when she looked up, for standing at the lip of the bluff where Rattlesnake Rock had once cast its long shadow, was a tall form. A man. Senor Garcia.

Angelica

Thank you, Rojo, for wanting to save me. Thank you, my love. But you must run. The man is coming back from the front of the truck and he would not return if he did not think he could beat you. He must have a weapon.

Go now, my dear one, before it is too late. You cannot save me and will only put your own life in danger if you try. Your concern should be your family, not me. You must go with them and ensure your herd is reunited and safe. That is your responsibility, your priority. A futile attempt to save me will only hurt them further.

But thank you for trying, Rojo, and fare thee well.

Senor Garcia

"I'll be right there. Don't let her get away," Senor Garcia yelled down to the slaughterer.

The man turned away from the fleeing stallion, his pistol in his hand. He waved to Senor Garcia, signaling he'd heard.

The ranch owner stepped up into the saddle. "Let's go, Macho," he said and reined the black gelding along the edge of the bluff. They'd go down a safer section of the decline.

As the gelding cantered along, Senor Garcia stared off into the horizon, his forehead lined with irritation. The fleeing girl, the one helping the blonde girl, was Jose's daughter. And here he'd been so concerned for her safety, thinking she'd been injured in the slide. What a fool he was, so worried she'd been hurt, when in reality, she was betraying him!

She would pay for her actions, and not only her, but her family too. There was no way he'd put up with such disloyalty on his ranch. As soon as the driveway was passable, they'd be gone.

Rosa

Rosa bent over the mare's ebony mane and threw her arms around the solid neck. The mustang rolled her eyes back and faltered for a moment, then straightened out and continued her headlong flight across the desert.

"Whoa, amiga. You have to stop. I have to go back. They won't catch you if you stop for just a second. That's all I need. Just enough time to get off."

But the mare didn't slow, nor did she falter again. Rosa looked back over her shoulder. Senor Garcia and Macho were gone from the top of the bluff. Had the ranch owner ridden down to help Senor Domingo with Angelica? What would they do with her?

"Whoa. Whoa," Rosa crooned, trying once again, though she knew it probably wouldn't do any good. She was right. It didn't. The mare simply ignored her and galloped on.

Senor Garcia

When Senor Garcia arrived, Senor Domingo was leaning on the closed back door of the truck, a cigarette held in trembling fingers and the gun lying on the fender just a few inches from his right hand. Senor Garcia didn't blame the man for feeling shaken. He'd never known such a strange day himself.

"Where is she?" he asked as he dismounted.

Senor Domingo motioned with an unsteady hand. "In the back." He stepped away so Senor Garcia could throw the door open. The girl lay just inside, sprawled across the dirty floor, her hair white and brittle. She didn't move.

"What did you do to her?" the ranch owner asked, his voice hard.

"Nothing. Nothing," Senor Domingo quickly replied. "I grabbed her, that's all. And I let her fall to the ground once, but she'd already fainted by then. I don't know what's wrong with her."

Senor Garcia looked down on the smaller man, his face lined in thought. He believed Senor Domingo. But now what were they to do?

"Uh, Senor," Senor Domingo said, interrupting his thoughts. "There is the little matter of money. You realize that I must have a refund? Of course, you do.

The mustangs did not leave your ranch, therefore they are still in your possession."

Senor Garcia turned fierce eyes onto the slaughterer. The man was insufferable. Not only did he allow himself to be fooled by a child and a teenager, but he expected his money back.

But then, it doesn't matter if I give him a refund. I'll get my money back, he thought. Jose's daughter is responsible for freeing the mustangs, so I'll deduct their cost from his wages before he leaves. He looked at the prone girl, his eyes hard. And this girl should pay as well, this girl with the strange white hair.

Rosa

The horses galloped on for miles, racing over the desert with a new breeze at their backs. Rosa wondered how they could go on for so long. If only they would tire. If only her mount would slow enough for her to jump, and then the stallion not trample her when she landed in front of him. But instead, the mare ran steadily onward, her nostrils flaring and sides heaving, her filly at her side.

It wasn't until the two foals began to lag behind that the herd dropped into a slow canter, and finally Rosa's mare fell into a fast, jarring trot. The girl clung to the tangled mane and tried not to bounce too much as she collected her courage to jump.

But there was no need for her to make that leap. The herd stopped suddenly, their heads raised as they peered off into the distance with sharp eyes. Rosa didn't waste time. Within moments, she was on the ground. The mare shied away from her as she landed, and like a shadow, the filly followed her, her eyes wide with alarm.

"Sorry," apologized Rosa. "I look scarier on the ground, don't I?"

A loud whinny pierced the air. Rojo was calling out. But to whom? Then Rosa saw a gray mare gallop toward them. Linda! And right behind her came Vivo and others. Tears sprang into Rosa's eyes, tears of happiness. The herd was being reunited! The horses galloped together, nickering joyously. Linda sidled up to Rojo, and Vivo and his sister greeted each other, then approached Bonita, their ears pricked forward as they welcomed the newcomer to the herd. The black yearling rushed to the bay mare Rosa had ridden and nuzzled her and the filly.

"A mom and her two kids," said Rosa. Her eyes turned to Vivo and she smiled sadly. "I hate to leave you again, amigos, but I have to go. Angelica needs me."

She turned toward the ranch and steeled herself. It was so far. She would be hours walking and running the entire way home. And what would she do when she got there? How would she save Angelica from Senor Garcia? Rosa started to run. She could figure that out as she went.

A familiar whinny came from behind her and Rosa stopped short. The cremello colt was gazing after her.

"Goodbye, Vivo," she said, her voice hushed. The colt whinnied again and Rosa felt tears fill her eyes. This would be the last time she'd ever see her wild horse friend. How terribly she was going to miss him! But at least he was safe now. At least, he was free.

With tears spilling down her cheeks, she spun around and ran. Not just toward Angelica, but away from Vivo – and away from the pain of a friendship that could never be.

Senor Garcia

Senor Garcia opened the kitchen door. The girl's mother, Senora Fernandez, was standing on the other side of the long wooden table, kneading dough on the floured surface. She stopped when she saw Senor Garcia.

"May I help you, Senor?"

"Si," said Senor Garcia. He searched the Senora's face. There was no duplicity there. The woman didn't seem to be hiding anything from him. But it made no difference. They had to go.

Suddenly, he became aware that Senora Fernandez was waiting for him to speak. He cleared his throat. "There's a girl outside," he continued. "Carlos is carrying her to the bunkhouse for now. I wish you to attend to her."

"What's wrong with her?" the Senora asked as she wiped flour from her hands.

Senor Garcia shrugged. "She's unconscious. I'll phone for the doctor after I contact the police."

"The police?" She sounded shocked.

"She freed the mustangs, and then collapsed."

"Oh my," said Senora Fernandez. Her hand went to her mouth. "And she did this all by herself?"

The tinge of admiration in her voice grated against Senor Garcia. Was he really the only one who saw the mustangs as pests? He noticed with satisfaction that his housekeeper left a smear of flour on her chin when she dropped her hand. "One of the mustangs must have kicked her," he said, ignoring her question. When Jose returned from his day's work, he would tell them about their daughter together. Right now, he needed Senora Fernandez's help with the mustang thief.

The girl's mother turned to a cupboard behind her and pulled out a first aid kit. "I'll see what I can do."

Senor Garcia stepped aside to let her bustle out the door. A horse's neigh sounded from the ranch yard, then quiet permeated the room. The dough lay like a fleshy lump on the table. The horse neighed again. Louder.

Accusing him.

"Shut up!" He clenched his hands into fists. What was wrong with him? The horse was just a horse, and horses neighed. It wasn't accusing him. How stupid!

This was all that strange girl's fault. She was the one who'd corrupted his employee's daughter. It was she who had freed the mustangs. He wouldn't be surprised to find out she'd made the horses act calm while being ridden too. And she was the one who'd created the dust horse. He couldn't forget that. It made sense that another of her powers was putting these bizarre thoughts into his head.

But no more. He left the door hanging open as he stormed toward the bunkhouse. It was time to confront her. When she awoke, he would be there, and he would accuse her for a change.

Rosa

Rosa ran for fifteen minutes across the desert before the thought she didn't want to think finally forced itself to the forefront of her mind. The necklace. She had to use the necklace. It would take far too long to run all the way back to the ranch.

But what if it drains away all my energy? The last time felt terrible, as if it was using up my life! And I don't even know if it'll work.

But then I didn't think it would be strong enough last time, and Angelica still appeared, she remembered.

With a sigh of resignation, Rosa sat down and squeezed the necklace between her fingers. "Angelica, come to me," she whispered. "You need to get away from Senor Garcia. You need to come to me one more time. Please."

She gasped as the energy drain struck her. There was the tug at her center, but this time it was far more intense – as if someone was yanking on a string threaded through her heart!

Be strong. Do it for Angelica.

And suddenly a part of her was stretching far, far away.

Be strong. Be strong.

The tendril of her being was stretching almost beyond endurance. She was growing thin. More than anything, she wanted to pull back. Retreat. Save herself. And she knew she could, if she chose to do so.

But Angelica saved me by putting me on the mustang. She had time to leap onto the mare's back, but she chose to save me instead.

Rosa sagged to the ground, unable to sit up straight any longer. What if she was pulled away from her body? What if she was stretched too thin and could never return to her normal state?

But I have to do it. I can't just leave her to Senor Garcia. What if he phones the police? They'll say she's a horse thief and she'll be sent to prison. I can't let that happen. I can't just abandon her.

Senor Garcia

Senor Garcia followed Senora Fernandez into the bunkhouse. She turned puzzled eyes to him when she saw the albino girl, then sat on the chair beside the bed and felt the girl's head for injuries or bumps. Swiftly and expertly, she checked the rest of her body. Finally, she turned to Senor Garcia.

"Senor, I can find nothing wrong with her," she said. "She's obviously very weak, but I can find no injuries at all. If she were kicked by one of the mustangs, there would be a mark. A scrape. A bruise. Something."

Senor Garcia nodded, relieved. At least the strange girl wasn't on death's door. He wanted her to be punished for freeing the mustangs, but he certainly didn't want her to die.

The woman touched the girl's forehead again. "She's neither hot nor cold. And while her breathing is faint, it seems a normal rate." She looked up at Senor Garcia, her forehead creased. "I don't understand."

"Surely the doctor will know. Phone him when you go back to the house and I'll send someone to meet him at the rockslide. The driveway is blocked."

"Would you like me to come back and sit with her afterward?"

Senor Garcia shook his head. "No, I'll keep an eye on her."

"Si, Senor." The woman moved to the door.

"Senora Fernandez."

"Si, Senor?"

"I wish to speak with you and your husband later this evening."

Her face told him she was shaken by his request "Of course, Senor," she said, her voice firm and confident. She turned toward the door with poised movements.

He was impressed. She was a strong woman. And her daughter was a strong-minded girl. Should he fire her parents simply because they couldn't control her? How would it affect their family to leave the ranch?

But that wasn't his problem. He couldn't have people around him he couldn't trust. The girl had been involved in freeing the mustangs, and she should be willing to suffer the consequences of her actions.

He'd always been willing to suffer the consequences of his own, on those few occasions he'd been wrong.

Rosa was only half aware that she was gasping for breath. Only half conscious that she was sprawled across the desert sand with the cacti and sagebrush looming over her. The other half of her was standing beside a bed in a dark room with shadows. One of the shadows moved like her mother. A warm, rosy glow surrounded the shadow's heart as her mother moved to the door of the room and disappeared.

Another shadow was shaped like a man with stiff bearing. Senor Garcia. His heart-light glared through the darkness, severe and unforgiving.

And beside him, on a dreamlike bed, lay Angelica, a rainbow light the size of a candle flame flickering over her heart.

Angelica. Rosa felt too weak to do more than think the word.

The girl's eyelids fluttered.

Come back to us, Rosa thought to her. *I summon you. Come with me.*

The room was growing darker. And Angelica was growing darker too. Already, the multifaceted light over her heart had shrunk to a tiny match light.

The room began to fade away and Rosa looked up desperately. Senor Garcia was becoming more blurred, the edges of his shadow more obscure. And then the tension in her own heart eased just a bit. It took her a moment to realize she was returning to her body in the desert, whether she wanted to or not. The necklace's power was gone. The magic that linked her to Angelica was finally depleted.

Angelica!

But the girl didn't move, didn't rise up to follow – and Rosa powerlessly withdrew, overcome with sadness, knowing she didn't have the means to save her friend.

Senor Garcia

"Rosa?" The spoken word was soft, almost inaudible.

Senor Garcia looked down sharply. The albino girl had spoken, had said her young accomplice's name.

"Do not leave me."

"She's not here," he said, and was surprised at how belligerent his voice sounded in the stillness of the room.

There was a long pause. "Senor," the girl finally said, speaking slowly as if the mere act of forming words took every bit of her strength. "To steal... a life... is a terrible thing."

"They're just mustangs!"

The girl turned her head slightly to the side and opened her eyes – her glowing, amber eyes – to look him full in the face. "To steal... a life is... a terrible thing," she repeated, her words almost too quiet to hear.

He stood speechless, mouth open, lost in her gaze. She seemed to be looking right through him and he squirmed under her scrutiny, wanting more than anything to escape. But he couldn't. He couldn't even look away. And as he stared helplessly into her golden eyes, he knew with a dreadful certainty that she could see every flaw in his character, every single selfish

159

thing he'd ever done in his life, every unkind thought that had crossed his mind, every brutal action – and yet she did not condemn him.

Then the strange girl closed her eyes and exhaled. He'd thought it was impossible for her to become paler, but she did. He held his own breath, waiting for her to breathe in again. And waited. Waited. Waited.

But instead of inhaling, she seemed to become smaller, to sink into the bedding. And he knew that the last bit of her precious life was drifting away. Before his eyes, her body was becoming a vacant shell, her life force was dissipating. She was dying.

Horror rose up screaming inside him, and finally free of her spell, he bolted for the door, desperate to get away from the growing barrenness on the bed. But there was no escaping the realization gathering like a storm in his mind.

The girl was right! He'd just seen the change at first hand – the irreversible emptying of a body as life left it. The vacant husk that remained.

The strange girl hadn't judged him for his actions before she died, but there was no need. His own shame condemned him. He knew he was guilty! How had he been so blind all these years?

And how many lives had he stolen?

Rosa

Rosa knew Angelica was gone before she rebounded fully into her body.

Goodbye.

The word echoed throughout her stretched being.

Thank you for trying.

"No," she whispered.

And someone else said *NO* as well. Not in words, but in spirit. A relentless flood of energy went crashing along the channels Rosa had forged, sweeping her up in it, and carrying her back to Angelica's shadowy room.

Rosa saw the girl gasp with renewed breath, saw her eyes open with golden light, and then, like magic, they were both swirling back to the desert spot where Rosa's body lay helpless.

Rosa

Rosa opened her eyes to a blue sky. A laugh came from her right and she weakly turned her head. Angelica was standing beside Vivo, her arms around his neck. The girl's hair was bright gold and her skin glowed in the sun. She looked perfectly healthy.

Was it my imagination? Did any of it even happen? Rosa pushed herself into a sitting position. She was so tired! And she felt weighed down, as if she was being dragged toward the earth. She fell back onto her elbows with a gasp.

"I am sorry, Rosa," Angelica said, rushing forward. "I should have removed the necklace as soon as I was able." She lifted the ice-cold chain from around Rosa's neck. Immediately, Rosa felt warmer. Lighter.

"What happened?" she asked, sitting up straight.

Angelica looked at her with radiant eyes. "You saved me," she said. "You and Vivo. I am so grateful."

Rosa looked up at the cremello colt with awe. "So it was he who... I remember a power..." Emotion choked her voice. "He helped me summon you."

"Yes," nodded Angelica, smiling brightly. "The necklace no longer held enough strength, but Vivo came to help you. Then he healed me."

"How? I don't understand."

Angelica knelt down beside her. "He sent his energy along the channel you formed and pulled us both here. And he was just in time. I was just passing over as he came. I could never have returned if that had happened. Then, when I appeared here, he cried over me. His tears of love healed me, a glorious gift."

Rosa looked up at Vivo with awe.

"I have something for you," said Angelica. "Another necklace. A new one." Her hair suddenly swirled in a hot desert wind, a wind that seemed to be touching only her. The golden girl reached up and twined one hair around a slender finger, and tugged. She cupped the hair in her palm and held it toward Rosa. "Take it," she prompted with a smile.

Rosa held out her hand, still speechless, and Angelica dropped the new necklace into her palm. It was warm and tingling, just like the first necklace had been at the beginning. Rosa breathed deeply when she slipped the magical chain over her head.

"Thanks," she whispered, finally finding her voice. She looked up at the colt. "And thank you too, Vivo," she said, and smiled when Vivo nickered in reply.

Rosa

Rosa skipped toward the ranch. The necklace around her neck added a wonderful warmth to her body and the knowledge that Angelica was only a call away added peace to her mind. They'd accomplished their task. The mustangs were out of harm's way and knew never to return. Angelica was safe and well. Ciervo was on his way to meet Rosa, or so Angelica said, so she wouldn't have to walk all the way back to the ranch. Now as long as Senor Garcia hadn't seen Rosa when she was galloping away on the bay mustang, everything would be almost perfect. And she was pretty sure he hadn't. Most likely, Rojo had grabbed his attention when he tried saving Angelica from Senor Domingo.

A short distance from the top of a small incline, she stopped to catch her breath. What an absolutely incredible day it had been. Not always easy, but definitely memorable! Only one thing, leaving Vivo behind, made her sad. But the sadness was bearable. At least she knew he was safe. He would live out his life without her, but it would be a long life, full of the pleasures given to mustangs.

She tipped her head back and closed her eyes. "Thank you, Angelica," she whispered to the wind and sun.

"Thank you for helping me, for saving the mustangs, and for letting me meet Vivo."

A pebble tumbled down the slope she'd just climbed, followed swiftly by another, and Rosa's eyes sprung open. Something was coming up the slope behind her. She spun around. With the brow of the hill in the way, she couldn't see, but she could hear something heavy climbing up the hill.

"Ciervo?" she whispered. Maybe they'd somehow passed each other and now he was tracking her, coming up behind her. She stepped to the edge of the incline to see exactly what she expected to see: a horse climbing the hill. But the horse wasn't a bay. He was a cremello. Vivo looked up at her and whinnied.

"Oh no," Rosa murmured. The colt lunged the rest of the way up the hill, sending small stones and pebbles spinning down the slope. On flat ground, he stopped and snorted. Rosa shook her head and stroked his white blaze. "What are you doing here, Vivo? You have to go back to your herd."

The colt sighed contentedly and moved closer to her.

"No, Vivo. You have to go back." She pushed his head away, and then with her hands on his neck, tried to turn him around. The colt merely turned his neck to accommodate her but didn't move his hooves. She stepped back and waved her arms, and he simply raised his head and looked at her with trusting eyes.

"Vivo, listen! Senor Garcia might kill you! Don't you understand? Don't you remember what Angelica said?" Her voice was desperate. He had to go back. She wouldn't let him risk his life again!

She picked up some pebbles and walked a few paces away, thinking she could gently lob them at the colt.

When he followed her, his head low and eyes apologetic, she dropped the pebbles in defeat.

"What am I going to do with you, little one?" she asked gently and stroked the soft neck.

"Let him come with you."

"What?" Rosa spun around to find Angelica standing behind her. "But Senor Garcia, you know what he'll do."

"Vivo knows the risks and still he prefers to be with you. You must allow him to make this decision."

"But Angelica… " Rosa stopped. Was this really a wonderful opportunity to keep Vivo with her always? Could she convince Senor Garcia to let her keep him? He had given the colt to her earlier that day. Maybe he was still feeling generous. And then she would see Vivo every day. She could take care of him and love him as much as she wanted and he deserved. But still, there was a risk, a huge risk, that Vivo might be hurt or worse – and it was a risk she didn't want to take. She shook her head.

Angelica put her hand on Rosa's shoulder. "If he tries to hurt Vivo, call me. I will come. Remember, you are not alone."

Rosa took a deep breath. "Okay." If Angelica would help her, she'd give it a try. As long as nothing terrible could happen to Vivo, as long as was safe, she'd face Senor Garcia.

Senor Garcia

Macho stretched near to the ground as he raced across the desert, Senor Garcia low on his back. The hot wind made the man's eyes water and the black's mane whipped back to sting his cheeks, yet the man encouraged the gelding to run faster. Faster.

But no matter how fast he raced, Senor Garcia's guilt didn't blow away. There was no escape from the vision of the dozens – hundreds? – of horses he'd sent to death.

One by one, they paraded through his mind. One by one – he wasn't sure how – he pictured them in incredible detail. One by one, he realized what he'd stolen from them.

When the last horse finally faded away, he flinched. The albino girl would appear next, he knew. She was the last one who's life he'd taken.

He almost cried aloud when Liana appeared in his mind. She stood and looked at him, her eyes sad, then opened her mouth to speak. He tried fruitlessly to shut out her voice, to not see her image, to think of anything else – but she could not be stopped. Her words simply spoke to every cell in his body, to every particle in his mind.

"You tried to steal my life too, Father, don't you see? You tried to steal my life by forcing me to be someone different than I am, someone who isn't me. And the only way I could save myself was to run away from you."

And Senor Garcia wept. Her words were true.

But maybe, just maybe, with Liana, he wasn't too late. Maybe she could still forgive him, maybe she'd allow him to make amends. Maybe, this one mistake, he could set right.

Rosa

Ciervo found them within minutes of Rosa and Vivo saying goodbye to Angelica once more. As she slid onto the gelding's back, Rosa couldn't believe how fortunate she was, how absolutely incredible life was. The possibility of two beautiful horses of her very own! She had to convince Senor Garcia somehow.

She squeezed her calves against Ciervo's side and the gelding leapt forward. Rosa laughed out loud in pure pleasure. Nothing could beat the wonder of riding her own horse across the desert, unless it was to have another horse friend galloping behind!

She noticed the dark mass in the distance the moment she topped yet another rise. A moment later, she heard the sound of men whooping and cattle lowing, the rumble of more than a hundred hooves pummelling the earth. The ranch hands had found the missing cattle, and from the direction they were traveling, it looked as if they'd been found in the foothills. Rosa reined Ciervo to a halt. One of the men waved to her, and though he was too far away to see clearly and she didn't recognize the horse he was riding, she recognized the wave. Her father. She waved back.

Her father left the herd and rode toward her on his new horse, a young gray Rosa remembered was named Steel. The sight would've normally made her feel sad, but not now. Bonita was safe. The elderly mare would live out her life with her new family, the mustangs.

"Ola, Papa," she called in greeting when he came close.

"What are you doing way out here, Rosa? You should be home, in bed after being so sick yesterday. And where did you find that horse?"

"Uh, he followed me," said Rosa, unprepared for the question. She needed to think of a better reason to have Vivo with her before she talked to Senor Garcia.

"A wild horse followed you?" His voice was full of scepticism.

"Si," said Rosa.

Her father's face darkened. "That's enough joking, Senorita," he said. "Now where did you find him? What do you have to do with the mustangs?"

Rosa hardly knew where to start. Obviously, her father didn't know anything about the events of the day. When he'd left that morning, the mustangs were in the corral at the ranch, not miles away. Bonita was in the barn waiting to be transported to her death, and she and Rina had been asleep in their beds. She was still wondering where to start when she noticed her father was staring past her with a startled look on his face. She turned on Ciervo's back to see a black horse galloping across the desert.

"It's Macho and the boss," her father said. "I wonder what's wrong. They're going so fast."

Macho came to a sudden sliding stop and his noble head turned toward Rosa, her father, and the horses. Rosa could see the panic in Senor Garcia's movements as he tried to turn Macho away from them. But the horse refused to go. He was listening to another

170

directive. Taking the bit in his teeth, he walked steadily and calmly toward the small group.

Expectantly, Rosa cast her gaze about. Yes, there she was, in a glimmer of gold on top of that distant rise. Angelica! This was her doing. And Rosa knew why. The enchantress was giving Rosa her opportunity to plead for Vivo on the open desert where the colt could easily escape, if need be.

She bit her lip. She wasn't prepared. The black horse was drawing near and she wasn't remotely ready. She'd thought she'd have time to make up a speech, but instead, she had about thirty seconds.

What could she say to the hardened ranch owner that would actually make a difference?

Rosa

Macho stopped in front of Rosa and Ciervo, bobbed his head and snorted. An uncomfortable silence spread among the humans. Rosa had never seen Senor Garcia at a loss for words. Something else was different about the man too, very different. His bearing, usually so stiff and unbending, seemed slack. He looked older and more tired than she'd ever seen him. And there were tears on his cheeks.

Now is the time. Talk to him.

The necklace around Rosa's neck tingled as the words sounded in her mind. She knew where the voice was coming from. And Angelica was right. Now was the time to talk. But what could she say?

Tell him how you feel. Trust me.

"Senor Garcia," Rosa started. "I think…" She stopped, tongue-tied. Her old shyness was back, and it seemed twice as strong.

But I have to talk to him. I have to do it for Vivo. And for all the old horses. For the mustangs that wander onto his land. "Senor Garcia, I think you're wrong when you sell the mustangs to kill them."

"Rosa!" Her father sounded shocked.

She turned to him. "Papa, I have to say this. And I know you feel the same. Almost everyone on the ranch does." She looked back at Senor Garcia and tried to

172

catch his eye, but he was looking down at Macho's mane. "I think you're wrong to kill the old horses too, Senor. There's nothing wrong with Bonita. She's as healthy as Ciervo and has a lot of wonderful years left to live. It's terribly cruel to discard her because she reaches a certain age. And even when she can't do what you want her to do anymore, you should realize that she's worked her whole life for you. She deserves to retire, to be cared for, and to be paid back for her years of effort with kindness. Not sent off and killed!"

"Rosa…" Senor Garcia said her name quietly.

"And what about Vivo here?" Rosa said, motioning to the cremello colt. She couldn't stop. If she did, she may never work up the courage to start again. "Vivo's a smart horse, and he's really nice. He deserves the respect due to all living things. All the mustangs are brave, strong horses. They're a lot more important than a little more grass, just so you can have a few more cows, to make more money that you don't even need!"

"Rosa," he repeated a little louder.

"Senor," she implored him. "I ask you to please, please, please, stop killing the horses. Don't run them off your land. Just let them live in peace. Let the old ones retire. Don't send them to their deaths just because they aren't useful to you. There are more important things than money."

"Rosa!" Senor Garcia and her father spoke as one.

In the silence that followed, Rosa looked in Angelica's direction. The new teardrops in her eyes stopped her from seeing the enchantress, but she was sure Angelica was still there, ready to act to save Vivo. Breathlessly, she waited through the long silence that followed.

"You're right." The ranch owner's words were quiet. "And I know it doesn't sound like much, but I'm sorry. If I could apologize to each of those I've harmed, I would. If I could bring them back, I would. As it is, there are only two things I can do; apologize to Liana and beg her forgiveness for being such a blind, hard-hearted fool, and I can treat the horses on my ranch well."

Rosa stared at him and her father's jaw dropped.

Senor Garcia didn't notice. "I've made many mistakes in my life, but one I've never made is to continue a wrong course of action after I realize my error." He looked up at Rosa, then his gaze shifted to her father. "I trust that you will tell no one of this conversation?"

Rosa's dad shook his head mutely.

"Of course we won't," Rosa added. For a split second, she marveled that she no longer felt shy with Senor Garcia.

"I'll do what I can to right my wrongs. There is little I can do about the past, but one thing I can do now is designate Lost Canyon as theirs, the mustangs' and the retired ranch horses'."

Rosa almost laughed out loud she was so surprised. The mustangs could return! And she had no doubt Angelica would tell them their perfect refuge was available once again.

"And I vow to both of you," continued Senor Garcia, "that I will never knowingly harm another creature, not animal nor human."

"And Vivo? Can he stay?" Rosa's heart raced as she waited for the answer.

"I gave him to you earlier today, and he's still yours, as long as your parents agree. And Rosa, thank you for freeing the mustangs. Otherwise, I would have their deaths hanging over my head now as well."

"You freed the mustangs?" Her father's voice was full of admiration.

Rosa nodded. "I had to, Papa. My friend and I..."

"Rosa," Senor Garcia interrupted her. "About your friend, the one who helped you."

"What about her?"

"I am so sorry, but your friend, the blonde girl, she... she..." Senor Garcia closed his eyes. "This one thing I cannot bear to say. This I will never forgive myself for," he murmured. "And I owe her so much. I owe her everything."

"Senor," Rosa said gently. "Angelica is fine. Look over there." She pointed. In the distance, the golden girl waved.

"What? But she... I saw... I don't understand."

A sudden brilliance burst around the enchantress and Rosa threw her hand over her eyes. Moments later, she cautiously lowered her shield. The hilltop was bare. Angelica was gone once again.

Rosa looked from the empty horizon to see both Senor Garcia and her father lower their hands and look at her with identical bewildered expressions.

But she had no answers. She'd never understood Angelica herself. "She can do cool things like that," Rosa said with an apologetic shrug.

And when, after a stunned moment of silence, both men laughed – Senor Garcia with immense relief that Angelica was alive and her father at Rosa's understatement – she laughed with them.

*I can hear you, Nefret. I can hear you, Aswan. And I
can feel the strange malaise that is falling over you.
I am coming! As quickly as I can, I am coming!*

What will happen next?

Please turn the page
for a sneak preview
of the next book

Sobekkare's Revenge

Available at:

www.ponybooks.com

Jumana

When an ancient treasure is unearthed in an Egyptian cave by a poor man named Abdullah, he becomes rich beyond his dreams. But one artefact among the riches carries a terrible secret. Queen Sobekkare placed a curse upon it thousands of years ago, a fatal illness that attacks only horses.

Abdullah's horse is quickly infected, and then the sickness spreads across the desert.

Jumana is shocked when she discovers her family's prized horses are missing. She follows their tracks into the desert, only to find them with a very strange girl who asks her to undertake a very strange task: stop the curse by finding the artefact and returning it, before it is too late.

www.ponybooks.com

CPSIA information can be obtained
at www.ICGtesting.com
Printed in the USA
BVOW08s0723051117
499590BV00020B/369/P